Dear Reader,

Welcome to Wyoming and the world of the Randalls. This family has grown a lot since Jake Randall first began his matchmaking. And each and every new Randall has his or her story. For the first time, I'm telling the story of a Randall woman. Although born a Randall, Victoria worries she might not have the heart of a Randall. But when challenged by circumstances, she fights for her family, her future and love, though she doesn't realize that marriage will ultimately be her reward.

Unfortunately, there's sadness along the way, but the family unites to withstand the difficulties they face. Just as they share happiness they also share grief. Fortunately, I can see into the future for my characters, and you know who will have his happy ending when *Randall Wedding* is published this December.

And please look for my next Randall installment, *Unbreakable Bonds*, a special Harlequin single title, coming next month.

Happy reading,

Judy Christenberry

Dear Reader,

Heartwarming, emotional, compelling...these are all words that describe Harlequin American Romance. Check out this month's stellar selection of love stories, which are sure to please.

First, the BRIDES OF THE DESERT ROSE continuity series continues with *At the Rancher's Bidding* by Charlotte Maclay. In the delightful story, a princess masquerades as her lady-in-waiting to save herself from an arranged marriage—and ends up falling for a rugged rancher.

Also available this month, bestselling author Judy Christenberry's *Randall Honor* resumes her successful BRIDES FOR BROTHERS series about the Randall family of Wyoming. Although they'd shared a night of passion, Victoria Randall wasn't in the market for a husband...and Dr. Jon Wilson had some serious romancing to do if he was going to get this Randall woman to love and honor him!

Next, when an heiress-in-disguise overhears a handsome executive bet his friend that he could win any woman—including her—she's determined to teach him a lesson. Don't miss *Catching the Corporate Playboy* by Michele Dunaway. And rounding out the month is *Stranded at Cupid's Hideaway*, a wonderful reunion romance story from talented author Connie Lane, making her series romance debut.

This month, and every month, come home to Harlequin American Romance—and enjoy!

Best,

Melissa Jeglinski
Associate Senior Editor
Harlequin American Romance

Judy Christenberry

RANDALL HONOR

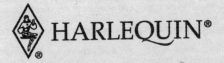

TORONTO • NEW YORK • LONDON
AMSTERDAM • PARIS • SYDNEY • HAMBURG
STOCKHOLM • ATHENS • TOKYO • MILAN • MADRID
PRAGUE • WARSAW • BUDAPEST • AUCKLAND

ISBN 0-373-16930-2

RANDALL HONOR

Copyright © 2002 by Judy Russell Christenberry.

This edition published by arrangement with Harlequin Books S.A.

® and TM are trademarks of the publisher. Trademarks indicated with ® are registered in the United States Patent and Trademark Office, the Canadian Trade Marks Office and in other countries.

Visit us at www.eHarlequin.com

Printed in U.S.A.

ABOUT THE AUTHOR

Judy Christenberry has been writing romances for fifteen years because she loves happy endings as much as her readers do. A former French teacher, Judy now devotes herself to writing full-time. She hopes readers have as much fun reading her stories as she does writing them. She spends her spare time reading, watching her favorite sports teams and keeping track of her two daughters. Judy's a native Texan, but now lives in Arizona.

Books by Judy Christenberry

HARLEQUIN AMERICAN ROMANCE

THE RANDALLS

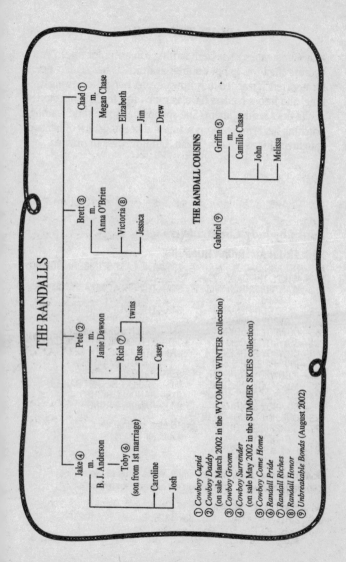

Jake ④
m.
B. J. Anderson
— Caroline
— Josh

Toby ⑥
(son from 1st marriage)

Pete ②
m.
Janie Dawson
Rich ⑦ ⎫
Russ ⎬ twins
Casey

Brett ③
m.
Anna O'Brien
Victoria ⑧
Jessica

Chad ①
m.
Megan Chase
Elizabeth
Jim
Drew

THE RANDALL COUSINS

Gabriel ⑨

Griffin ⑤
m.
Camille Chase
John
Melissa

① *Cowboy Cupid*
② *Cowboy Daddy*
(on sale March 2002 in the WYOMING WINTER collection)
③ *Cowboy Groom*
④ *Cowboy Surrender*
(on sale May 2002 in the SUMMER SKIES collection)
⑤ *Cowboy Come Home*
⑥ *Randall Pride*
⑦ *Randall Riches*
⑧ *Randall Honor*
⑨ *Unbreakable Bonds* (August 2002)

Chapter One

Dr. Jonathan Wilson opened the door of Randall Accounting, a grimace on his face. Two days in town and he already had to deal with a number cruncher. Not his favorite thing.

But Dr. Jacoby had insisted.

He'd expected life to be different here. After all, Rawhide, Wyoming, was a lot smaller than Chicago. He supposed he'd been unrealistic. Everything always seemed to come down to numbers, or maybe he should say dollars, even in this small town. After years of med school, he should know that.

"May I help you?"

The cool, educated voice snapped him out of his thoughts. Sitting in the large reception area, a petite blonde greeted him.

He guessed something else was the same as in Chicago. Beautiful women hovering near money. He'd bet this woman wouldn't be able to tell a debit from a credit. She was there to find out who had money and how she could get some.

"Russ Randall, please," he said briskly. He'd

learned his lesson from his poor father. Avoid blond leeches if at all possible.

Her delicate eyebrows lifted slightly, as if she heard disdain in his voice. Not a way to make friends in this small town.

"I'm sorry, he's not in right now. May I take a message?"

Jon was surprised that Randall had such professional help in a small town. She sounded almost as businesslike as he. "When do you expect him back?"

"I'm not sure. Could you tell me the nature of your business?"

She really was quite beautiful, but then his mother had been beautiful, too. Beautiful, greedy and self-centered.

He tried to find a pleasant way to refuse to answer. He didn't want to make her mad. Finally he said, "It's private."

Any friendliness he'd imagined he'd seen disappeared. Her face expressionless, she said, "Russ is at lunch. He'll return in about an hour. You may wait, or I'll ask him to call you." Without waiting for an answer, she picked up a pen and turned to the papers on her desk.

He stood there, feeling the coldness of her manner. He pulled out a piece of paper from his pocket. "Is there someone who could show me the apartment he has for rent? It had this same address."

Her head came up and she stared at him. "Who sent you here?"

"Why? Is the apartment a secret?"

"Dr. Wilson, we're normally a little more open in Rawhide. You might want to make a note of that." She opened her desk drawer and pulled out some keys. "This way."

"How did you know who I am?"

"Certainly not from your friendly greeting."

She'd circled him and was going out the front door. He decided he'd better follow her. He could determine her source of information later.

The accounting office appeared to occupy half the ground floor of the small building. The other half was a newspaper office. According to the sign painted on the window, its name was the *Rawhide Roundup*. Oh, yeah, that would probably be the same as the *Chicago Tribune* with hard-hitting news and in-depth articles about scientific discoveries.

He sighed but kept going, following in the blonde's wake, unconsciously noting her trim behind in nicely tailored slacks.

At the edge of the building, she turned a sharp left and began climbing a stairway that ran up the side of the building.

He peeked over the railing as he climbed and saw what looked like a parking lot behind the building. "Is there parking back there?"

"Yes."

Okay. She was mad at him. Good thing she wasn't going to be his landlord. She'd never let him move in in the first place.

She reached the landing and then turned left again, going to the front of the building. She paused in front of two doors and unlocked the door on the right. She walked inside and folded her arms over her nicely formed chest. Not that he noticed.

"The apartment has two bedrooms and two baths, a full kitchen, including a microwave, refrigerator and dishwasher. The floors are hardwood in here, but the bedrooms are carpeted. There's no air-conditioning, but it has gas heat, and the fireplace is gas."

She remained in the center of the room, looking as unfriendly as ever.

"Thank you. May I look around?"

She sighed. "Of course. I'm returning to our office. Please lock the door when you leave." Then she walked out.

And he still didn't know who she was or how she knew his name.

Victoria Randall muttered several words under her breath in reference to the man she'd left upstairs. Her mother, Anna, had stopped by the office yesterday, bragging about the new doctor in town. According to Anna, the man was brilliant, handsome and single.

She'd have to take her mother's word on two out of three of those traits. Anna worked part-time as a nurse and midwife in the area, so presumably she'd know.

He was handsome, all right. But Tori knew he was a snob and unfriendly. He'd thought he was dealing with a receptionist, and he was much too important to even introduce himself. And he was going to be her neighbor?

She reached the office and sat down at her desk, trying to fix her mind on the work at hand. She had a lot to do. Business was good. After she'd gotten her accounting degree and the C.P.A. designation, she'd studied for her broker's license, too. Their offices, hers and Russ's, offered full financial services.

She'd bought in as Russ's partner after Bill Johnson had died. He'd had the original practice and Russ had become his partner. When Bill passed away, Russ had bought the office building and the accounting business from his widow. That big an investment had made things difficult. He'd been pleased when Tori had expressed an interest in investing with him.

So, she decided, blowing out a long breath, she should've told the doctor who she was. Why had she reacted as coldly as she had? That wasn't the way she was.

The office door opened and she looked up, expecting the doctor to have returned. Instead, she greeted her uncle, Griff Randall.

"Hi, Uncle Griff."

"Hey, Tori. I was in town and thought I'd stop by to see if you'd read the Kiplinger letter yet. They just recommended the stock we bought last week. That endorsement should make the stock go up."

"Yes, I did this morning." She grinned. "Our timing was perfect."

"I think we should hold on to it for a while. Its profit-to-earning ratio is good."

"Very," she agreed. "Let me show you something if you have time. I've been looking at another stock." She turned to her computer screen and quickly brought up some research she'd done.

Griffin had been a broker in Chicago before he came to Rawhide. His mother had been her father's aunt, but she'd left Rawhide as a pregnant teenager and no one had heard of her again. In the end, she'd asked her son to bury her on the Randall ranch.

When Tori had expressed an interest in the stock market as a teenager, her father had suggested she talk to her uncle Griff, who now lived on a neighboring ranch. He'd been her mentor ever since.

Griff circled the desk and was leaning over Tori's shoulder to see the information she'd found when the door opened again and the doctor returned.

Tori stiffened and said, "Yes? Do you have any questions?"

"Yes, several. But don't let me interrupt."

Even though she was irritated with him, Tori couldn't bring herself to be rude. Especially not in front of Uncle Griff. "Dr. Wilson, this is my uncle, Griffin Randall. Uncle Griff, this is the new doctor in town. Dr. Jonathan Wilson."

Griff reached out his hand and the doctor shook it. "Glad to meet you. I hear you're from Chicago."

The doctor appeared surprised that Griff knew that information and Tori shook her head. He had a lot to learn about small towns.

"Yes, I am."

"Me, too. Born and raised there."

"So you're visiting?"

"No. I live here now. Once Rawhide gets its claws into you, you never leave."

The handsome man raised his eyebrows. "I will. I'm returning to Chicago in four years. I'm required to stay that long."

Both Tori and Griff were surprised. At least, Tori guessed at Griff's reaction when he asked the next question.

"Why four years?"

"It's a government program. They offer interest-free loans to med students if they'll work four years in rural areas after graduation."

"And then you'll just abandon the town?" Tori asked, her voice rising in horror. Doc Jacoby, the current doctor, had been in Rawhide for almost forty years. He wouldn't be retiring now except that he was old and tired. He said he wanted to spend his sunset years fishing and visiting with friends.

"I'm sure the government will find someone else to do four years," the doctor said, showing no concern for Tori's reaction.

There was an uncomfortable silence. Then Griffin said, "Maybe you'll change your mind."

The man gave a brief smile, not the least bit warm, and said nothing.

"Do you want to leave a message for Russ?" Tori asked abruptly.

He looked at his watch. "I think I'll get some lunch and come back. According to what you said earlier, he should be here in about half an hour, right?"

"Approximately." Russ usually had lunch with Abby, his wife, at the elementary school. He'd be back when Abby's afternoon class started, but Tori didn't feel like sharing any personal information with the new doctor.

"All right. Thanks." The doctor started turning toward the door when Griff stuck out his hand.

"Glad to meet you, Dr. Wilson. Hopefully my family won't be in too frequently."

"Of course, glad to meet you, Mr. Randall. Anytime I can be of service." Then he nodded to Tori and left the office.

"As long as it's within four years," she said, mocking the man's words. "And probably not unless it's convenient! I can't believe that jerk is going to replace Doc!"

Just as she finished her complaint, the door opened again and the doctor reappeared. "I forgot to ask. Is the other door another apartment?"

Her cheeks flushed, she nodded.

"Is it rented?"

"Yes," she snapped.

"Will I have nice neighbors?" he asked.

She couldn't believe his nerve. He wouldn't be a nice neighbor. How dare he expect better than he'd give?

Griff gave her a quizzical look. Then he answered the doctor's question. "You bet. Your neighbor is the cream of the crop."

"Great. Thanks."

When they were alone again, Griff said, "I gather

you didn't bother to inform him that you live in the other apartment.''

"No. It wasn't any of his business. He hasn't rented the apartment yet.'' She sighed, then said, ''I didn't mean to be rude. But he wouldn't even introduce himself. How's he going to replace sweet old Doc?''

"Doc deserves his retirement.''

"I know, but…you're right. Hopefully, I won't get sick in the next four years!''

"I'll vote for that. Say, can you print those pages so I can take them home and look them over? I'll call you tomorrow.''

"Sure.'' As the pages were being printed, Russ came in. After greetings all around, Tori gave Griffin the pages and he said goodbye.

"Anything happen while I was gone?'' Russ said as he shrugged out of his jacket.

"Yes. Our lovely new doctor came to see you.''

"Oh? Well, that's not a surprise. Doc asked me to hold the apartment for him.''

"Well, I think you should rent it to the first drunken cowboy you can find!''

Russ froze, staring at his cousin in astonishment. "Why?''

"Because he's awful! Cold and stiff. Rude. And he's leaving in four years, like the people don't matter!''

"I know. Doc told me. But he's hoping he'll decide to stay. Doc figures he will get him married before the time comes for him to go.''

"Fine! Just make sure my name's not on the potential-wife list!"

"Wow, he really ticked you off, didn't he?"

"You'd better believe it. I wouldn't—"

The door opened again. She was grateful she'd stopped when she did. She didn't like the man, but there was no point in announcing that to him.

"Mr. Randall?" the doctor said, as he closed the door behind him before extending his hand.

"Yes, make it Russ. You'll soon find there are a lot of Randalls in this neck of the woods," Russ told him warmly.

Tori kept her gaze down, fighting the urge to tell him not to waste any charm on this jerk.

"Thanks, Russ," the man replied, his voice as friendly as Russ's.

Tori stared in surprise. Had he had a personality change in half an hour?

"Your receptionist showed me the apartment and I definitely want it. It's very nice."

"Good. I'm glad you liked it. But Tori—" Russ began.

The doctor interrupted. "Could we talk in your office?"

"Sure. This way." Russ gave Tori an apologetic look over his shoulder.

ONCE THE DOOR to the office was closed, Russ offered his guest the chair in front of his desk. "Please, sit down."

Jon did so, relaxing. He liked this man. He felt

comfortable with him, which was more than he could say about the sexy blonde in the front office.

"Before we go any further," Russ said, still smiling, "I think I should tell you that Tori is my cousin."

Jon pursed his lips, glad Russ had made his relationship to the blonde clear. Not that Jon had intended to insult the woman, but he had considered complaining about her behavior. For Russ's sake. He probably thought the woman was perfect.

Russ wasn't finished. "And an equal partner in the firm."

"*She's* an accountant?"

"Has her C.P.A. and her broker's license."

Jon stared at him, trying to take in that information. And Dr. Jacoby thought these people should do his bookkeeping for him? He thought he'd better find someone else. "Well, that's wonderful. I definitely want the apartment. Can we discuss terms?"

"Of course."

Jon appreciated the way the man did business. He told him what he charged for rent, explained all the details and then waited.

"Sold! When can I move in? I'm staying with Dr. Jacoby right now, and I'd like to get settled in." As he asked that question, he drew out the new checkbook he'd gotten from the bank that morning and began writing a check for the deposit and the first month's rent.

"The apartment's ready and I'll hand you the keys right now. It's a couple of days until the first, but I'll throw those days in for free. Welcome to Rawhide, Doctor.''

"Oh, call me Jon. It's easier.''

"Great, Jon. I think my wife will be one of your first patients.''

"I'll look forward to meeting her.''

Russ sat there, smiling, as if waiting for something. Had the old doctor told him he'd be doing Jon's books? Uneasy, Jon stood. "Well, I'll probably start moving in tomorrow. My things will be here day after tomorrow.''

Russ looked surprised, but he nodded and said, "Let me know if I can help you with anything.''

"Thanks.'' Then Jon headed for the door. He'd explain to Dr. Jacoby why he hadn't hired the Randalls to do his accounting for him. Maybe the older doctor could patch things up with Russ for him.

AFTER THE DOCTOR LEFT, Tori appeared at Russ's office door. "Well? Did he take it?''

"Of course he did. There's not much else in town for rent.''

"And are we doing his books like we do Doc's?''

Russ chuckled. "Like *you* do Doc's books. But no, he didn't mention that. So it looks like you'll have a little more time for that investment project you wanted to do.''

Tori stared at him. "But who is he going to use? There's only Abe Forsman. He's the biggest gossip in town. He'll blab everyone's illnesses all over the place! Doc would never—''

Russ held up his hand. "Not our choice, Tori. Besides, we're not hurting for business. In fact, we're going to have to hire someone to sit out front and get you set up in the other office. We could use a good secretary."

"But I don't know who we'll get. Most of the high school and college kids have already gotten summer jobs."

"No, I don't mean summer jobs. I want us to get someone permanent."

"But I can't think of anyone looking for work right now." She knew most everyone in Rawhide.

"We'll find someone. Spread the word. Maybe someone has a relative who'd like to move here but is worried about a job."

"We could take out an ad in the paper, too."

"Only if you write the ad. I'm not that good with words, just numbers."

"Ha! You're just saying that. But I'll do it. Maybe if I take it over today, Joseph will put it in the weekend paper."

"Good thinking!"

"Do you want to see it before I take it over?"

"Nope, I trust you, partner. I'm going to be busy modifying the ranching program for Hector Scott's place."

"Okay. Oh, by the way, did you tell the good doctor that I live in the other apartment?"

"No, he didn't ask." He frowned. "You're not worried about him living next to you, are you? He seems like an okay kind of guy."

Tori chuckled. "No, that's not the problem. I just don't think he'll make a pleasant neighbor."

"I told you Doc's planning on marrying him off before his four years are up. Are you worried about the women parading in and out of his apartment?" Russ asked with a grin.

Tori had been raised with all her boy cousins. Teasing was nothing new to her. "Not hardly. In fact, please make it clear to all the family that I have no interest in the man."

"Now, honey, that would be like waving a red flag in front of Uncle Jake's face. If you're really not interested in him, you'd better keep that under your hat."

Russ closed the door to his office, ready to go to work. Tori stood there staring into space. Unfortunately, Russ was right. Uncle Jake wouldn't rest until he saw all the Randall children married.

So she'd keep her distaste for the doctor secret…as long as her family was around.

But upstairs, Dr. Jon Wilson would feel the brunt of her disdain for a snooty doctor from Chicago.

Chapter Two

Jon left the clinic at noon the next day. He headed to the café in the same block as his apartment and had a quick lunch, keeping his eyes open for the arrival of the rental truck he'd hired. The driver had told him he'd be there at noon.

Over an hour later, he flagged down the driver and directed him to the parking lot behind the building. Jon hoped he'd be able to pay the man a little extra to get him to help carry his belongings upstairs.

"No way, man," the driver said gruffly when Jon asked him. "I got to return the truck and head for Chicago as soon as I can." While he was talking, he was unloading Jon's belongings and setting them down on the gravel of the parking lot. "I could use some help here."

"But—"

"I'll hand this out to you," the man said, ignoring Jon's attempt to persuade him. In half an hour, Jon stood in the middle of the parking lot, all his belongings around him, watching the truck drive away.

"Great. If I go back to the clinic to ask Doc where

I can hire some men, everything will be gone by the time I get back.''

After thinking a couple of minutes, he decided to risk going to the accountants' office and borrowing their phone.

The blonde, Victoria, was at her desk.

''Uh, may I borrow your phone for a minute?'' To his amazement, she slid the phone closer to him without asking any questions.

As he dialed the number to the clinic, Russ Randall came out of his office. ''Well, hi, Jon, how are you?''

Since the number he dialed had a busy signal, he hung up the phone. ''Frustrated.''

''What's the problem?''

''All my belongings are sitting in the parking lot. At least they are if they haven't been stolen. I was calling Doc to see if he knew where I could hire someone to help me, but his line is busy.''

''I should've thought to offer. I'll help. And if you'll give me a few minutes, I think I can round up some others,'' Russ said calmly.

''I can pay—''

''Don't be silly,'' Russ said, and turned to Victoria. ''Call Rich. Then try the house. Maybe Toby didn't ride out today.''

''Sure.'' She pulled the phone back toward her and dialed.

Since she wasn't looking at him, Jon admired her beautiful face. He didn't know what kind of worker she was, though he was beginning to think she wasn't like his mother. But he knew for sure she was beautiful.

"Ready?" Russ asked, distracting him.

"Uh, yeah, but I hate to take you away from your work."

"I can use some exercise," Russ said, and led the way out of the office.

TORI WATCHED THE TWO MEN go out while she was calling. When Red asked what she needed, she explained the situation. He immediately agreed to find Toby. He also offered one of the chocolate cakes he'd just finished making. When Tori protested, he said he could bake another one before dinner.

She hung up the phone, a smile on her face. Her family was wonderful. They pitched in for everyone.

She started back to work, not thinking about the doctor. She was determined to keep her distance from that man.

An hour later, she answered the phone to discover Doc's voice on the line.

"Hi, Doc, how's retirement—"

He interrupted her. "Get Jon. We've got a wreck on the highway with multiple injuries. Your mom is on her way. I need him as soon as possible."

"Right." She hung up and ran out of the office around to the parking lot. The guys had moved a lot upstairs, but there were still some things in the parking lot.

"Where's the doctor?" she demanded.

"Just went upstairs with Casey, carrying some boxes. Anything wrong?" Rich asked.

"Multiple accident. Doc needs him," she called over her shoulder as she raced up the stairs.

She found him in the living room and hurriedly repeated the message.

With a worried frown on his face, he thanked her and ran out of the apartment. She stared after him, revising her opinion of him. At least he seemed intent on his job, even if it was for only four years.

"People are hurt?" Casey asked.

"I guess so. They called Mom in, too."

Russ, Rich and Toby came up the stairs, the three of them carrying a beaten-up sofa. Russ puffed out some air. "I'm not sure this sofa is worth the effort. What do you think, Tori?"

She grinned. "I've seen worse."

"Where?" Rich asked when he let go of the sofa.

"At college. I'm sure the doctor couldn't afford expensive furniture at med school. In Caroline's letters to Aunt B.J. she says she never gets back to her apartment anyway. It sounds like they work them twenty-four hours a day."

"I've seen that on TV, but I wasn't sure that was the truth," Toby said. "Elizabeth likes that show, *ER*."

"Have you seen a table? For the breakfast area?" she asked, staring at the empty space.

"Nope. He really doesn't have much. But we still have some boxes of books. Talk about heavy!"

"Maybe we should tell him about the table and

chairs Aunt Megan took in last week. She didn't want to put them in the store. She was hoping to find someone to take them off her hands," Tori pointed out.

"Hey, good idea," Russ said. "They weren't bad, just not old. Aunt Megan only wants antiques in her store. Maybe Abby and I will give him the table and chairs for a housewarming present."

"You're going to give him a present because you're his landlord?" Tori asked. "Do you think that's necessary?"

"Not necessary, no, but I think it would be nice," Russ said.

"Anybody home?" Red's voice called.

They all turned around to find him standing on the doorstep, Mildred right behind him.

"Come in, Red. The doctor's not here. He had an emergency," Toby said.

"We heard. It was bad. They had a couple of fatalities," Mildred said. "I talked to Anna."

They all lamented such a horrible accident. Then Mildred asked Tori to put the lasagna in the refrigerator. "We thought the man could use some dinner that's already prepared. I'm sure he won't have any groceries yet."

"That's so thoughtful, Mildred," Tori said.

"Here's the chocolate cake, too," Red said, extending his offering.

"I know he'll appreciate it, Red." Tori put the cake plate on the bare cabinet.

"I guess he'll get in late tonight. Maybe Elizabeth and I will buy some groceries to fill up the pantry for

our housewarming gift,'' Toby said. "I'll call her.''
He pulled out a cell phone and moved away from the
rest of them.

Tori moved to the door. "Well, I left the office
unmanned. I'd better go back.''

Russ stopped her. "Go lock it up and come help
us. No man should come in late from that kind of
work and find everything a mess. Poor guy doesn't
have a wife.''

"That would be a good way to get to know him,
Tori,'' Mildred suggested, enthusiasm in her voice.

Uh-oh. The Randall family was famous for its
matchmaking, but Tori didn't want any part of it. Especially with a man who was leaving in four years.
"No, I don't think I can spare the time.''

"Sure you can,'' Russ insisted. "Abby will come
by after school, and she'll help you.''

Toby joined them again. "Elizabeth will be by, too.
She and Abby agreed to do some grocery shopping.''

Tori was feeling trapped, but at least she wouldn't
be alone. And it would be terrible to find everything
just dumped after dealing with a horrible wreck.
"Fine. I'll go close up.''

Once she'd locked the doors downstairs, leaving a
note on the door, she went back up the stairs. The
main bedroom had a nice bedroom suite all put together. It looked new, with its king-size bed, dresser
and bedside table. When she started opening boxes,
she found one marked "bedroom'' and opened it. Inside were a set of new sheets, and a navy comforter

with flecks of maroon forming a pattern. Very masculine.

"I'll take the sheets to my apartment to wash before I make up the bed. Want me to bring back a pitcher of lemonade?"

Her cousins enthusiastically agreed to that offer.

When she returned, she brought the lemonade, along with what cookies she'd had in her cookie jar. She knew her cousins' appetites. Especially Casey, Russ and Rich's baby brother. At eighteen, he was still a growing boy.

"I called Aunt Megan," she said as they fell upon the snack. "She said she'd be glad to donate the table and chairs just to get rid of them. She'll be there another hour if you want to go get them."

Russ stood up. "I think we can get them and be back here before the girls arrive," he said to Rich.

"No problem," Rich agreed. "I brought my truck." The two of them left.

"That sofa is a sore spot, isn't it?" Casey asked. "I mean, I'm no expert on decorating, but it's an eyesore."

Toby laughed. "You're right."

"I bet Mom and Dad would like to give him a new sofa."

"No," Tori said firmly. "We can't do that without asking him. And it isn't necessary for everyone to give him presents."

"Everyone gave Russ and Abby presents when they moved into their new house."

"Yes, but everyone knows them. No one knows

the doctor. He's a city man.'' She didn't want to say bad things about him.

"Poor guy,'' Casey said. "I'd hate living in a big city.''

"I think he prefers it. He's leaving in four years.'' She needed to keep reminding herself of that. As good-looking as he was, she felt sure he'd have a lot of feminine company while he was here, but she had no intention of involving herself in a temporary relationship. Especially with someone who didn't respect her.

Casey was still frowning.

"Are all the boxes up here?'' she asked, starting to open another one.

Casey groaned and Toby downed his glass of lemonade. "Come on, boy. The lady is cracking the whip.'' Both of them headed down the stairs.

Tori continued staring at the sofa. She suddenly remembered a sofa cover she'd used in college. It was royal blue and she thought it would fit the sofa. She hurried next door and searched through her hall closet. She brought it back to the doctor's apartment, along with several pillows in a blue, green and maroon print. The guys were making a second trip.

"Where did you go?''

"Over to my apartment. I'll have a surprise when you get back.'' As soon as they were out of sight, she slipped the cover over the sofa. It fit perfectly. Then she added the two pillows.

Toby and Casey entered the room, each carrying a

box. When they saw the sofa, they set the boxes down and stared.

"You found a new sofa?" Casey asked.

"Of course not. It's an old cover I used in Laramie." All of them had attended the University of Wyoming in Laramie.

"Nice job, Tori. It looks a hundred percent better."

"Thanks, Toby, but that scarred coffee table is the only other piece of furniture he has."

"Yeah," Toby agreed. "But maybe he'll buy some more soon."

"I think he should buy a TV. He's only got that little black-and-white thing," Casey said in disgust. "Man, he's really roughing it."

"You're spoiled, Casey," Toby told him, laughing.

IT WAS ALMOST TEN O'CLOCK when Jon returned to the parking lot. None of his belongings were still on the gravel. He didn't know if the Randalls finished the job for him, or if someone had come along and taken what they wanted.

He trudged up the stairs, bone tired. He hadn't had time to do any grocery shopping. Doc had told him to come back to his house tonight, but Jon was looking forward to puttering around in his own place. He'd skip dinner tonight and eat breakfast at the café in the morning.

Tomorrow was Friday. He'd have the weekend to settle in. He sighed. Hopefully there wouldn't be any more emergencies of the magnitude of today's crash for a while.

He placed the key in the lock and swung open the door. The interior was lit with the soft light of a lamp, inviting and warm. He smiled in pleasure. Then he remembered he didn't have a lamp like that.

Frowning, he reached for the light switch near the door. The kitchen was to his right, behind a wall, but there was a dining area after the kitchen. He discovered a table and chairs he didn't own.

Had he accidentally come into the wrong apartment? He looked around nervously. If he had, whoever lived here would think he was a burglar. He backed up until he was outside his door. Nope, there was the other door on the left.

What was going on?

He entered his apartment again. This time he made it to the living area. The ugly sofa he'd inherited from another med student had been replaced with a royal blue sofa, the same shape, but with colorful pillows on it. It almost looked fashionable. And there was a stuffed chair and ottoman that he didn't own. A floor lamp with a built-in round glass table cast a soft glow about the room.

He went to the biggest bedroom. This would tell the tale. If the bedroom suite that his father had given him as a graduation present was there, he was in the right place.

He let out a deep breath. It was there. But the bed was made, looking so inviting he had to fight himself to keep from falling into it. He went back to the kitchen. Figuring he could use his hands as a way to get a drink of water from the sink faucet. He at least needed that before he went to sleep.

Much to his surprise, he discovered his dishes, the few he had, all nicely stored in cabinets that had a shelf lining in place. There hadn't been any shelf lining there yesterday.

There was a note on the cabinet.

"There's lasagna in the fridge. Put what you want to eat on a paper plate and microwave it for two minutes. There's a pitcher of lemonade, too. And Red made you a chocolate cake to welcome you to Rawhide."

His mouth watered when he caught sight of the cake. And lasagna? He opened the fridge and saw the square dish. He whirled around, ready to heat some up at once. Where were the paper plates?

He opened the pantry door and discovered fresh bread, many cans of food, coffee in a can to be perked and instant coffee in a jar that was caffeine free. And paper plates.

Who had performed this miracle? There was a teakettle on the back of the stove for heating water. He filled it at once and turned on the burner. Even though it was June, a good cup of coffee would hit the spot.

He heard the faint sound of a television next door. He went outside and knocked on his neighbor's door. If the guy had helped, or seen who had done this, he'd like to thank them.

He heard hesitant steps come to the door. He was all ready to ask his questions when the door opened.

Until he found himself facing Victoria in a long night-gown topped by a matching robe.

"Victoria! What are you doing here?"

"I live here. I'm your neighbor, Dr. Wilson." She didn't appear to be surprised.

"Why didn't you tell me?"

"It's none of your business where I live." She started to close her door.

"Wait! I want to ask you—" He stopped as he heard the kettle whistling. "I'm heating water. Can you come with me?" he asked, not waiting for an answer. But he was remembering several remarks by both Anna and Doc. In particular, Doc. Talking about what a cute couple he and Victoria made.

Once he was back in his kitchen, he got down a second cup and put instant coffee in both of them and added the hot water. He took both cups to the new table and put them down. His neighbor was just coming into his apartment. "I'm going to warm up some lasagna. Do you want some?"

"No, thank you. I'm about ready to go to bed."

"There's also chocolate cake. I don't know how good it is, but it looks delicious."

She hesitated, then said, "Thanks. I'll have a piece of cake. And it is delicious. Red made it."

Tori moved into the kitchen, noticing for the first time the weariness on the man's face. She'd talked to her mother and heard about the difficult day. She'd also listened to a lot of praise for the doctor's medical skills and also his concern for his patients.

"Here, I'll heat up the lasagna and cut the cake. You go sit down and drink your coffee," Tori said.

"Thanks."

She put some lasagna in the microwave and cut two pieces of cake. By that time, the lasagna was done. Taking it to the table, she slid it in front of the doctor, along with a fork. Then she went back for the two pieces of cake.

For several minutes, the doctor ate the lasagna. Then he looked up. "I have some questions for you."

"What?" Tori answered calmly.

"Who is Red?"

"Red's kind of our grandfather and Mildred's his wife, sort of our grandmother."

"Why do you say it like that? Are they or aren't they?"

"Red is a cowboy who raised my dad and his brothers after the youngest of them was born, after their mother's death. So he's family even if he's not really a Randall."

"And they brought this food over?"

"Yes, to welcome you to Rawhide."

"And the food in the pantry? The new furniture?"

"The chair and ottoman is from Aunt Megan and Uncle Chad."

"Randalls?"

She nodded. "The table and chairs are from Russ and Abby. The food in the pantry and the coffeepot are from Toby and Elizabeth."

"Randalls?"

She nodded.

"The sofa?"

"That's your sofa," she began, but he interrupted.

"That's not my sofa. My sofa is an ugly print that a dump wouldn't even want."

She put down her fork and walked over to the sofa. She slipped the sofa cover up so he could see underneath. "This is a sofa cover I had left over from college."

"I see."

"There's a homemade quilt on your bed, too. It's a gift from Rich and Samantha, his wife. She made it last winter, taking lessons from his grandmother."

"And she made up the bed?"

Tori felt her cheeks flush. "No, I washed the sheets and made the bed. We all figured you'd be too tired when you got in tonight."

"You were right, of course, but I didn't expect such generosity. I'll be glad to pay everyone for—"

"These are gifts, Dr. Wilson. We're not asking for money. Everyone wanted to make you feel welcome, and to make your job easier. Life would be much harder for all of us if we didn't have a doctor here. Surely you know that."

"I know that I'm not going to work for free. So I don't expect anyone to give things to me. While I appreciate the thoughtfulness, it makes me feel obligated to your family."

"Obligated? You think we're going to want free medical help?"

"It happens to doctors all the time. If I go to a party, people ask me to diagnose a spot on their arm.

Or a sore muscle they got from running, so they won't have to go to an office and pay for professional care.''

Tori ground her teeth and took a deep breath. ''I can assure you, Dr. Wilson, that my family will not refuse to pay for medical care. If you talk to Doc, you'll discover that we pay our bills on time! Or maybe you should ask his accountants. Oh, wait, that's me!'' She gave him a fierce glare.

''Look, don't take offense, but this isn't normal in Chicago. I'm uncomfortable with all this.''

''So I can see. But we're not from Chicago, and things are different in Rawhide.''

''I know they are. That's why I want to make everything perfectly clear. No matter how much your family does for me, or gives me, and no matter how many 'wifely' things you do for me, I have no intention of marrying you.''

Without another word, Tori stood and walked out of the apartment.

Chapter Three

Jon got up at six the next morning, having had a good night's sleep, thanks to the Randall family. He regretted what he'd said to Victoria the previous night, but he had to clear things up before the family did more for him. He wasn't sure why Victoria was hard to marry off—she was certainly beautiful and hard-working—but Doc and Anna were certainly working hard to get him interested in her.

At least he knew she wasn't like his mother. But he had no intention of marrying her. In four years, he was going back to Chicago. Back to a normal way of life.

He fixed his own breakfast before he headed to the clinic. He wanted to check his patients first thing this morning.

After doing rounds, he was pleased with the progress his patients had made. The clinic was completely full, with two beds to each room. A couple of the people could have gone home, if they'd lived in Rawhide, but none of them did, so all twelve were tucked away.

He told the nurses he was going back to his apartment and run some errands and would return at ten. He needed to buy a phone and plug it in so he could be reached if needed. And he wanted to talk to Russ Randall about his accounting needs. He hoped there wouldn't be any problem about him and Victoria, now that he'd explained himself. Otherwise he didn't know what he'd do.

Doc had explained that the only other bookkeeper in Rawhide wasn't reliable or trustworthy. So that left his landlord. He liked Russ, but they had to have everything clear.

The accounting office opened at nine o'clock, and he was waiting when Victoria came down the stairs from her apartment. She didn't even speak to him or acknowledge his presence in any way. He followed her into the office.

"Good morning, Victoria. When does Russ get in?"

"When he wants to." Her words were cold and she didn't look at him. Obviously, she was unhappy with him.

"Victoria, I didn't mean to upset you last night. I just wanted everything clear. Doc and your mom—"

"You achieved your goal. However, marrying you was never my plan. You have no need to worry."

He was about to question her when the front door opened and Russ entered. "Jon! How'd you manage last night? Everything to your satisfaction?"

"It was wonderful, but I was a little embarrassed about all the help."

"Don't be ridiculous. We just wanted to make you welcome. I figured yesterday was a tough one." He grinned, then asked, "Are you here to see me or Tori?"

"You, please, Russ, if I may, before I go back to the clinic."

"Sure. Come on in."

Once he was seated in front of Russ's desk, Jon got right down to business. "I need to hire you to do my books."

Russ grinned. "Doc must've told you about Abe. He's a nice old man, but he does love to talk."

"Yeah. I hope you won't hold it against me that I wanted to check things out before I made a commitment." That was a nice way of saying they weren't his first choice.

"No problem. We're kept pretty busy by our regular customers."

"But you'll take me on?"

"Sure. Tori has a system worked out that—"

Uh-oh. Here we go again. "Russ, I want to be clear about this. I want *you* to handle everything for me. Not Victoria."

For the first time he found a less than cordial look on Russ's face. "Why?"

"I don't have a lot of faith in women accountants, especially one as pretty as your cousin."

Russ continued to frown. "No one ever complains about working with Tori. She's brilliant."

"Look, I'll be brutally frank. I think your family has lined me up as your cousin's future husband, but

I have no intention of marrying while I'm here. I'll be glad to return the gifts I received yesterday, except the cake and the lasagna. I'm sorry, but I'm going to remain a bachelor as long as I'm in Rawhide.''

Russ stared at him. ''You think—but we were— have you said that to Tori?''

''I didn't want any misunderstandings,'' Jon said stiffly.

Russ threw back his head and roared with laughter. ''Oh, mercy,'' he finally said as his chuckles lessened. ''Is she mad at you?''

''Oh, yeah. No woman likes to be rejected. But it's not her…exactly.''

''Glad to hear it.'' He leaned forward. ''Listen, Jon, what we all contributed to your home yesterday was to welcome you. Nothing else.''

''But Doc and Anna—''

''Ah, well, I can't help what they said. Doc announced to the entire town he intended to get you married to a local girl so you'd stay instead of leaving. So you'll probably have a lot of women hitting on you. But I imagine that happens to most single doctors.''

By the end of that speech, Jon was frowning in consternation. ''I can't believe he did that!''

''Then you don't know Doc. Or this community. Matchmaking is a popular pastime.''

''I guess I'd better have a personal discussion with Doc,'' Jon said grimly. ''I thought it was just your family that thought—I apologize.''

''If it will make you feel any better, Tori has told

everyone she's not interested in marrying you. I think you're safe there.''

It surprised Jon that Russ's words didn't make him feel better. "Why?"

Russ appeared surprised, too. "Why? She didn't say. I don't think she's ready to marry. She'll only be twenty-four in September. She's got plenty of time."

Jon wasn't going to ask any more questions. He didn't want to convince her cousin he was interested in her. "Okay, good. Now, about my bookkeeping. You'll do it?"

"No."

His brief answer startled Jon. "Why not?"

"I do most of the ranching cases. I have some software that Tori's dad created. Tori does the retail stuff. And that includes Doc's business. You'll have to ask her to take you on."

"But I can't—" Jon stared at Russ, not happy with the alert interest in his eyes, the smile on his lips. "You're enjoying this, aren't you?"

"Somewhat. I suspect Tori may enjoy it even more. Especially if you made her mad."

"Oh, yeah, I made her mad. What do I do if she turns me down?"

"I don't know, man. Send her flowers?"

"But that would make people think I want to date her. Then I'm in trouble again."

"Yeah." Russ's grin grew even wider.

Jon huffed and puffed, but Russ didn't offer any other suggestions. Jon finally stood. "I might as well get it over with."

TORI WAS WORKING on the feed- and general-store books. The two sisters who owned it had signed on as customers over a year ago. Tori kept their books and issued paychecks for their employees. But she looked up when Russ's door opened. She hadn't forgotten who was in there with him.

"Tori," Russ said, a big grin on his face, "Jon wants to talk to you."

The look on Jon's face didn't say he was happy about that fact. She'd make it easy for him by turning him down at once.

"Sorry, I'm busy right now."

Dead silence followed her announcement, but no one moved. Finally she looked up.

The doctor didn't wait for any more encouragement. "I need to ask you to take on my accounting, like you do Doc's."

Tori shifted her gaze to Russ. He silently nodded, letting her know he thought it was a good idea. Of course he did! More income and no embarrassment. For him. Did he know what the doctor thought?

"I'm not sure that's a good idea, Dr. Wilson. I get the feeling you don't have much confidence in my abilities." She'd worked hard to be accepted as an equal to Russ.

"Your cousin and Doc both assure me you're more than competent. I'd appreciate your help."

She drew a deep breath. "I suppose I could...as

long as you realize our relationship is strictly business." Her voice had hardened as she finished. Okay, so maybe it wasn't nice to throw his words back in his face, but it sure felt good.

He cleared his throat. "I think that sounds fine."

"Fine," she agreed. Then she pulled a copy of a form she'd developed to set up an account. "Please fill out every blank on this form and mail it back to me. Then, at the end of each week, you'll turn in your patient files and I'll set it all up. I assume you'll be using the same scale as Doc?"

"Probably so. I'll check with him. Can I drop this off when I'm finished? It seems silly to mail it when I live upstairs."

"I thought you would prefer as little contact as possible. However, if you want to shove it through the mail slot, I'll handle it." She would prefer not to have any contact, just so everyone in town would get the hint.

"Thanks." He turned around and offered his hand to Russ. Her cousin shook it and thanked him for his business. Then he turned and looked at her.

After a moment's hesitation, he extended his hand to her, too. "Thanks for taking me on."

She shook his hand reluctantly. But she would be professional. "Of course. Let me know if there are any problems."

With a nod, he hurried out of the office.

"You were kind of hard on him, weren't you?" Russ asked.

"Do you know what he assumed when he discovered all we'd done for him?"

Russ shrugged his shoulders, telling her nothing.

"The arrogant man decided it was bribery to get him to marry me. It seems Mom and Doc have been pushing him in that direction!"

"He's not used to people being nice. He comes from Chicago. You remember, Caroline wrote Aunt B.J. about how cold and unfeeling everyone was." Russ folded his arms across his chest. "Give him some time, Tori."

"He can have all the time he wants, as long as he leaves me alone. I've worked too hard and long to convince people I'm as competent as you and not just a dumb blonde!"

Russ grinned. "I know. Even I didn't believe you could convince people, because you used to be so quiet. But you've learned to speak up for yourself."

"Yes, I have. And if that man dares to question my skills in any way, I won't be doing his accounting for him, no matter what kind of bind he's in. Do you hear me?"

"Yes, ma'am," Russ agreed, still grinning. He admired Tori's fierce determination.

IT WAS FRIDAY, the day she normally stopped by the clinic and collected the patients' pay sheets. She'd record the amount owed, print out a bill and mail it to the patient with a return envelope. The doctor never had to deal with the business end. It was a system that had worked well for Doc.

After Russ had arrived, she left the office and walked the two blocks to the clinic. Usually Tori enjoyed the walk. It helped remind her that it was Friday, the start of the weekend. And the exercise felt good. Today, she prayed she'd get the information from the receptionist and not have to see the new doctor.

"Hi, Faye," she sang out to the receptionist. "Do you have all the papers ready?"

"Not quite," the receptionist said. "Dr. Jon wants to see you first. He has a question."

"He should've had you call the office. It would have saved time."

"It won't take long." As she said that, Faye picked up the phone and called the doctor. "Doctor, Tori Randall is here."

She hung up the phone and smiled at Tori. "You can go to his office. It's Doc's old one. Doc is using that little room down the hall when he's in."

"I see." Without saying anything else, she opened the door to the examining rooms and office and went in. She lifted her chin and straightened her shoulders, determined to give the appearance of a confident, all-business woman.

He was waiting for her at his door. "Come in, Tori. I'm sorry to take up your time but I have a couple of questions."

"Next time you should have Faye call me. It would save both of us time."

He let one eyebrow slide up as if he doubted that comment. He invited her to sit down and circled the desk to sit in Doc's old chair. "Doc said sometimes some patients don't have insurance and need payment plans. He said you take care of that for him. Do you know the people well enough to do that for me? I'm not sure who can afford to pay and who cannot."

"If you want me to discount rates or set up payment plans I can. I know most of the patients well enough to make those determinations."

"Good. That's what I'd like."

She stared at him. "Just like that? No calling and asking permission from you?"

"I have to trust you, Tori. Doc says you're trustworthy."

"I'll remember to thank Doc," she said, her voice cold, recognizing that it was Doc he trusted, not her.

"I also forgot to ask when I get a statement about the money deposited in my account." When she said nothing, he added, "I don't want to write a lot of rubber checks."

"I make deposits on Fridays. They'll send you a copy of the deposit, probably on Tuesday. You can ask Doc when it comes in."

"Great. Uh, if—if I discover a patient who can't pay at all, can I mark NP on it, or just not send the billing to you?"

"I'll need that information for your tax records, so it would be in your best interest to send the billing. If NP is what you want to use, that works for me." She paused, then added, "But it will take you longer to pay off any debts you have from medical school if you do that."

"Thank you, Miss Genius Accountant. Even I can figure that out," he assured her, a grim smile on his lips.

She gave him an abrupt nod and stood up to leave.

"Tori? I was wrong. I apologize. Can't you forgive me?" He stood there, tall, handsome, a charming smile on his lips.

Which only made Tori madder. She'd bet he always got everything his way because of that smile. "I'm trying to be professional, Dr. Wilson. Like people in Chicago."

She heard him sigh as she closed the door behind her. But she had no intention of relenting and smiling in return. That would only confirm his suspicions.

On the walk back to the office, she decided she couldn't be friends with him until he had at least a girlfriend or, preferably, a wife. So she'd start looking for a good candidate.

When she returned to the office, Russ was coming out of his, grabbing his jacket off the hall tree that stood by the front door.

"Where are you going?" she asked, expecting him to tell her he was meeting a client.

"Something's wrong. Abby was supposed to go to school today. They were having a meeting to discuss a special project they're starting for the fall. She didn't show and she's not answering the phone."

Something in Tori's head sounded an alarm. Abby loved teaching. Besides, she was always on time and always responsible. "I'll go with you," she said, putting the papers on the desk.

"She probably overslept. She hasn't been feeling good lately. I'm sure everything's okay."

"Probably, but she might be sick and need some help. I'm coming," Tori told him, leaving him no choice.

Russ had bought ten acres of land just outside town, so it was only a five-minute ride. They'd built a beautiful house. Abby called it her dream house. Though the family had protested they should live on the ranch, like the rest of them, with both their jobs in town, they'd graciously refused.

As she fastened her seat belt, Tori asked, "Why hasn't she been feeling well? Has she seen the doctor?"

"Yeah," Russ said, but he didn't add any details.

"Well? What's wrong?"

"I'm not supposed to tell," he said, but he was grinning.

Tori guessed at once. "She's pregnant!"

"Yeah, but don't let on you know, or she'll kill me. We had a hard time and she wants to wait a little longer before she tells the family."

"Russ, that's wonderful. I figured it wouldn't be long since Rich and Samantha are expecting. Oh, that's great. How far along is she?"

Russ was still beaming. "About two and a half months. She said we can tell everyone at three months. I've been dying to tell Mom and Dad."

"So she's been throwing up every morning? I almost got sick myself when Samantha described her first three months." She shuddered.

Russ frowned. "No. But she's been getting bad headaches. Since school ended, she's stayed in bed when they happen. But she won't take anything for it because of the baby. I convinced her to go see Jon and she's got an appointment Monday."

"Maybe she should go see Doc Jacoby. You know, she's used to him."

"She's already seen him once."

"But I didn't see the billing."

"She paid him cash and asked him not to let you know," he told her with another grin.

"The sneak!" She knew Russ would know she was teasing. Abby was like another sister in the sprawling Randall family.

He turned into the driveway of his new house. "Life is just almost too good, Tori," he muttered. "Abby, the new house, now a baby." He opened his door. "You want to wait here?"

"No, I'll come with you. But I won't say anything about the baby," she promised.

"Be sure you don't. I don't want her mad at me. She'll put me in time-out like she does the kids at school!"

Tori ignored that comment. Russ and Abby were so in love. They…completed each other, more than any people she'd ever seen. If he had to go to time-out, Abby would go with him. They did everything except their jobs together.

Since he had company with him, Russ pushed the doorbell as he unlocked the door. "Abby? Tori and I are here. Are you dressed?"

An eerie silence was the only answer. Tori frowned and followed Russ into the foyer. The house was curiously quiet.

"Maybe she's still asleep," Tori suggested.

"I'll go check. Wait here."

Tori pretended to study the furnishings in their new house. Abby had great taste and Aunt Megan had helped her decorate the house. Even though Russ hadn't given her a budget, not wanting to deny his beloved Abby anything she wanted, Abby had used some family antiques she'd had from her parents, who were both dead now. And she'd bought some things from Megan's store. She'd even gone to estate sales and auctions with Megan. The result was an eclectic collection of nice pieces. Very personal.

She could hear Russ's voice calling Abby's name. Again there was no response. Russ came back down the hall, looking into the different bedrooms.

"I'd better check to see if her car is here. Maybe Elizabeth picked her up and they stopped to shop before the meeting. She's probably there already. I'll look in the garage and you call the school, see if she's turned up there."

The closest phone was in the kitchen, the favorite room in the house, always filled with sunshine in the mornings. The door to the garage was off the kitchen, so she followed Russ across the den in that direction, praying he was right.

Something didn't seem right to her.

Russ had his eyes focused on the left, going to the

garage. Tori turned to the right for the phone. She was the one who saw Abby first.

"Abby!" she screamed.

Russ spun around. He saw his wife lying on the floor, not moving.

He ran to Abby's side, wrapping his arms around her.

Tori grabbed the phone and called 911. Saying it was an emergency, she asked for a doctor. After she gave the directions, she asked for her mother, but her mother wasn't working that morning.

Russ was kneeling on the floor, rocking Abby in his arms, tears streaming down his face.

Tori lifted the phone again and dialed the Randall ranch. Her mother answered the phone. "Mom, come quick to Russ's house and bring Janie. There's something wrong with Abby."

Chapter Four

Abigail Randall was dead.

It didn't take a genius to know that. Jon was pretty sure Russ knew that, but he had to tell him anyway. He was going to transport her body back to the clinic. He turned and entered the den where Anna and another lady sat with Russ.

"Russ," Jon said gently. His gaze met Tori's first. She was standing behind the couch. Finally Russ looked up at him. Jon could tell he was still in shock. His movements were slow, his eyes glazed.

"Yes?" he whispered.

"Your wife has…passed away. I'm going to take her back to the clinic and try to determine what happened."

Russ continued to stare at him. "She was pregnant."

"I know, Doc told me."

"Russ?" Rich Randall shouted as he came through the door. He didn't know what was wrong, but his mother had called his house on the way to Russ's. As his twin, Rich probably felt the closest to his brother.

Jon turned and caught Rich by the arm. Whispering, he said, "His wife died. I'm taking her away now. He's in shock."

It appeared Rich was in shock, too. He stood there, his mouth open.

Tori appeared on Rich's other side. "Russ needs you, Rich. Abby was—p-pregnant and—he was so happy."

Anna moved from Russ's side, leaving room for Rich to comfort his brother. She came to Jon. "Is there anything I can do to help? She was so young!"

He squeezed Anna's arm. He wanted to offer comfort to Tori, too, but he didn't feel he could. "I know. I'm going now. But Anna, I want you to keep an eye on Russ. He's in shock. If he needs medication to sleep, let me know, okay?"

"Of course, but I can go to your office if you need me."

He knew she meant to help on the autopsy, but he wouldn't ask that of her. "Thanks, Anna, but I'll manage. I'm very sorry for the family's loss." His gaze traveled to Tori, also, but she didn't look at him.

The phone rang. Tori looked at her mother. "Shall I get it?"

Anna nodded.

Jon watched her step to the phone. She was a strong woman. His mother had always expected every crisis to revolve around her, but Tori was different.

"Uncle Pete, Abby—Abby's dead. We found her collapsed on the kitchen floor. The doctor's about to leave. Aunt Janie, Rich and Mom are here with Russ…yes, I'll tell her.''

She told her aunt Janie that Pete was on his way, then turned back to her mother. ''That phone is going to start ringing off the wall,'' she murmured.

''I know.'' Anna gave her a steady look. ''Can you handle the phone? We sure don't want Russ having to do that.''

''Yes, of course. I'll find a pad and pen and make a list.''

She walked away and returned as the phone rang again, the necessities in hand.

''She's very composed,'' Jon muttered to her mother.

''Yes. We aren't used to tragedy. We've been very fortunate. But we're strong. Don't worry. We'll take care of Russ.''

He nodded. ''If there's anything I can do, let me know.''

ABBY'S FUNERAL WAS HELD Sunday afternoon. The rest of Friday and Saturday, Tori handled the phone, answering curious questions and talking to all Russ's and Abby's friends. Everyone was shocked at Abby's sudden death.

Dr. Wilson, in his secondary role as medical examiner, had let them know that her death was caused by a brain hemorrhage. She'd died instantly and nothing Russ could have done would have changed the outcome. Tori hoped those words comforted her cousin. They helped her, but it was such a waste of a good person. Abby had been so happy to be a part of the huge Randall family. Thrilled to be pregnant.

Tori tried not to think about the loss, but it was impossible not to. She constantly teared up. On Sunday afternoon, when they buried Abby, she stood with the family, lined up with Russ in support, to say goodbye to Abby. It was a difficult time.

She was worried about Russ. He had a blank stare and never spoke. His parents had convinced him to return to the ranch to sleep, giving him a room in the main house so they could insure he got rest and decent food. And that he wasn't constantly reminded of his dead wife.

Tori closed the office on Monday, but opened it on Tuesday. She thought staying busy would be the best thing to do. She spent part of her day talking to people who stopped by to commiserate with Russ, and accepting potted plants from people who hadn't heard before the funeral and wanted to express their sorrow.

She was closing at five when Dr. Wilson came to the door. With a sigh, she opened the door. "Yes, Doctor? I'm just closing."

He gave her a sympathetic look. "Busy day?"

"Yes. Do you have more questions?" Her voice was strained from her exhaustion, but she couldn't help it.

"I wanted to check on you and see how Russ is doing."

She was surprised, but she'd been checked on so much the entire day, frequently by people wanting to share in the drama even if they hadn't known Abby, she couldn't stand it any longer. She used her standard answer. "Russ is doing as well as can be expected."

"Which tells me exactly nothing. Have you been using that expression all day?"

"Yes."

Instead of demanding more detail, he asked to borrow the phone. He had a pager and a phone in his SUV, but he didn't carry a cell phone. She nodded and he picked up the receiver and dialed. When he received an answer, he asked for Anna.

"Hi, it's Jon. How is Russ doing? Does he need some help?"

Tori had talked to her mother that morning, but Russ had still not arisen.

"He's what? Are you sure that's safe?"

"What?" Tori demanded, rising.

He shook his head at her. "Yeah. Well, let me know."

"What?" she asked again.

"Okay. I will," he said into the speaker, and then hung up the receiver. "Your mother is worried about you."

She shrugged that off. "What did she say about Russ? Is what safe?"

He studied her, making her angry. "Tell me," she demanded.

"I will if you'll have dinner with me at the café. I promised your mother I'd make sure you ate."

"Don't be ridiculous. You don't want to be seen in public with me. Gossip is rampant right now."

"Did you eat lunch?"

"There wasn't time."

"Well, there's time now. If you go upstairs, you'll be answering the phone all evening."

She groaned. "I don't think there's anyone left to call."

"I suspect there is. Come on, let's go get something to eat and I'll explain what your mother said." He didn't try to grab her arm and pull her after him, which one of her cousins might have done. He stood back and waited, leaving the decision up to her.

She suddenly agreed, knowing he was right. She'd get more calls tonight if she was home. And she just didn't think she could manage. She didn't want to go out to the ranch, as her mother had suggested this evening. She nodded. "I'll go, but I'll pay for my own dinner."

"Agreed. I love a cheap date." He grinned. His expression was such a relief, such a normal response, she almost broke into tears.

She looked away and picked up her purse. "I'm ready."

Grabbing the keys, she preceded him out the door and then inserted the key in the lock. As she was doing that, several people stopped to talk to them. She stood back and let Dr. Wilson handle the questions. But she did manage a sad smile as they offered their condolences.

"Thank you," she muttered as they crossed the street and entered the café.

Mona, one of the waitresses, came to seat them and

told Tori how sorry she was about Abby's death. Tori thanked her, but she said nothing else.

"Mona, we need a back booth. Tori's about worn-out from all the kind people here wanting to talk to her. As her doctor, I'm ordering a quiet meal with no interruptions."

Mona shot Tori a sympathetic look and smiled at the doctor. "I've got just the booth you want." She led them to the last booth and pointed out the side where Tori would be facing the back wall. "You sit here, hon, and I'll intercept anyone who thinks he recognizes you."

"Thank you, Mona."

Her escort slid into the other side. "Good for you, Mona. You deserve a big tip." Then, before Tori could assure him she'd pay the tip, he asked, "What's the special tonight? Meat loaf?"

"Nope, but we have it on the menu. Tonight, it's chicken and dumplings."

"Okay. Give us a minute to look at the menu."

When Mona left the table, Tori buried her face in her hands.

"Take deep, slow breaths and blow out all that tension."

She didn't hesitate to do as he suggested. She was desperate.

But then people began stopping at the table to express their sorrow.

"I never thought I'd hate being with a blonde," Jon muttered. "If you were a brunette, no one would notice."

Tori didn't bother answering. She was fighting for composure.

Mona came back to the table. "Sorry, I'm doing a lousy job. But my other tables are demanding service. You ready to order?"

"Yes, and we want everything boxed up to go. I'll have meat loaf with fried okra and mashed potatoes. And coconut cream pie. You want the same, Victoria?"

She didn't even know what he had ordered, but she nodded. As soon as Mona had it all down, he said, "I'll be back in ten minutes to pick it up. Thanks, Mona."

"Where are you going?" Tori didn't intend to sound so panicky, but she couldn't face any more mourners.

"You tell me. Your place or mine."

"What?" She didn't understand what he was asking.

"I say yours. It's sure to be nicer than mine. Come on, let's get you home."

She didn't argue.

He took her arm and led her across the street and up the stairs to their apartments. When they reached his door, he dug out his keys and opened the door.

"I thought you said my place."

"I'd forgotten about the phone. I hear it ringing now. You wouldn't be able to get any rest." He gently nudged her into his apartment. "Lie down on the sofa and rest. I'll go back and get the food."

Like an automaton, she did as he said without arguing. That took too much strength. As he left the apartment, she closed her eyes.

WHEN JON RETURNED to his apartment with several bags of food, he found Victoria asleep on his couch. Poor kid! She must've had an awful day. Several of his patients told him about talking to her. He figured she'd answered a lot of calls, but he hadn't realized how bad it had been. She was running on empty.

He allowed her a half-hour nap, then shook her shoulders. "Tori, let's eat before everything is cold."

"What?" She sat up, bleary-eyed, and stared at him.

"You've had a little nap, but the food is going to get cold. I've set the table, so let's eat."

He wondered how long it would take her to remember to ask what she wanted to know. They ate for five minutes before she put down her fork and stared at him.

"What did Mom say?"

"That's pretty fast recovery, Tori. Your mother said Russ is going camping in the morning…alone. He's said he can't deal with all the sympathy and talk about Abby. He needs to be alone to handle his grief."

"Alone? Can't he take Rich with him? Or someone?"

"Your mom said Rich offered to go with him, but he's insisting he wants to go alone. He's not really going to camp out. He's going to stay at a cabin. I can't remember the name of it."

"Potter's cabin?"

"Yeah. How'd you know that?"

"The brothers bought out a man named Potter about twenty years ago. The only building on his place was the house, no more than a cabin, and a falling-down corral. We've gone there in the summers to look for strays, sometimes to move a herd up there, but it's not good rangeland."

"Who are the brothers?"

That question made her open her eyes wide. "Sorry, I forgot you wouldn't know. We kids call them the brothers when we're talking about Dad, I mean, Brett, Jake, Pete and Chad. My three uncles. We call their wives the aunts."

"So Russ will be sleeping inside?"

"Yes. How long did he say he'd be gone?"

"A few days."

She frowned and said nothing. Today was Tuesday. So he'd leave on Wednesday and he would be back before the weekend was over.

"You think he'll be okay?"

Her head snapped up. "Of course…if he remembers to eat."

"He probably will."

"I hope so, but…sometimes, with what's happened, it's hard to remember it's important."

"Like you didn't eat lunch today?"

"One meal doesn't matter. I'm eating tonight." She avoided his gaze, sure he would remind her that she was only eating because he insisted. But she would've eaten something when she got home. The sound of the phone ringing next door warned her what was waiting for her.

"You finished?" he asked, drawing her attention again.

"Yes. Thank you for helping out tonight. I won't bother you anymore."

"Well, I appreciate that. But first you have to eat your pie."

"I ordered pie?" she asked in surprise.

"You sure did. Said you wanted the same as me. And either Mona wanted to justify that big tip, or they serve mighty big pieces of pie at the café."

"I forgot about Mona's tip! I forgot about paying at all. I'm so sorry. Here, I'll get my purse and—"

"Eat your pie. I gave Mona a big tip and you can buy next time."

He certainly knew how to distract a woman. "Next time? There won't be a next time. Don't you understand? If you're seen with anyone twice, the gossips in Rawhide will have you married to her within a week. In their minds, at least."

"Really? I don't think—" The phone rang. He excused himself and went to the bedroom. Then he returned to the door.

"It's your mom. She's worried about her little chick."

Straightening her shoulders, she glared at him before stalking into the bedroom. She sat down on the edge of the bed and picked up the receiver. "How did you know I was here?" she asked her mother.

"You weren't at home, and Jon promised he'd try

to get you to eat something, so I took a chance. How are you, darling?''

"It's been rough, Mom. The phone has rung off the wall, and I have enough potted plants at the office to start a garden. Does Russ—? I know he's leaving in the morning, but what would he want me to do about them?''

"I think he can't make decisions right now. I tried to convince Pete that someone should go with him, but he said he understood how Russ felt.''

"Oh, dear. I'll make a list of the senders, but I'm not sure I can keep all of the plants alive until Russ is ready to acknowledge everything.''

"Jess and I are coming in to the office tomorrow," Anna said at once. "I should've thought about you all alone there. Jessica and I can take turns answering the phone and watering the plants and making a list. I know you've got work to do.''

Tears pooled in Tori's eyes. "Oh, Mom, that would be so wonderful. Are you sure you don't mind? Jess is only here for a few weeks. Are you sure she'll agree?'' Jessica, her sister, had just finished her sophomore year at the University of Laramie. She always complained about how limited her time at home was.

"She won't mind. If she does, I'll remind her about when she had chicken pox and you spent your entire Christmas vacation reading to her and playing games with her when the other kids were taking sleigh rides and building snowmen. She owes you!''

"Oh, Mom! I'd really be grateful if you both could

help me,'' she said, trying to disguise the sobs she couldn't hold back.

''We'll be there. And I'm sorry about today. Now, let me talk to Jon, sweetheart. I love you.''

''I love you, too.'' She lay the phone down on the bed and went to the door. ''Mom wants to talk to you again,'' she said, sniffing to keep her voice clear.

He gave her a frowning stare, then passed her on the way into the bedroom.

She returned to her place at the table. The doctor had cleared away their dinners and set out two huge pieces of coconut pie. Since he'd already eaten half of his, she picked up her fork. Now that she knew she wouldn't have to face tomorrow alone, she had a little appetite for the pie.

He returned to the table and sat down again, attacking the rest of his pie.

Neither of them spoke until he finished his pie. As soon as he put down his fork, so did Tori. ''Thank you for dinner,'' she said. ''It was good and I appreciate the peace and quiet.''

''Good. By the way, your mom had an interesting idea for us. She suggested you spend the night with me tonight.''

Tori stared at him, her mouth open.

Chapter Five

Tori recovered quickly. "I don't believe you!"

"Well, I'll admit she didn't mean what you're thinking. But your mother and Doc haven't been too subtle, you know."

"Ignore them. Mom must not know you're leaving in four years."

Jon grinned at her. "She knows, but she and Doc seem to think you'd be able to change my mind." He stood. "I want you to know that won't happen. What your mother meant was that you should stay here, sleep on my couch and go back home early in the morning."

"Why would I do that?"

As if on cue, her phone rang faintly through the walls. Jon pointed his thumb in the direction of her apartment. "That's why."

"I'll just take the phone off the hook," she insisted.

"The phone company frowns on that. It will beep all night."

"Then I'll unplug all my phones!"

"And scare everyone when there's no answer? If they get the answering machine, they'll leave a message and you'll have a record of who called. I'll even give you the bedroom and take the sofa myself."

Tori was impressed with his offer. He was at least six feet compared to her five-foot-three-inch frame. "That would be absurd. You'd hang off both ends."

He shrugged. "Interns get used to poor sleeping conditions."

"It's not necessary—"

"Your mom is worried about you. She feels bad about leaving you alone to deal with everything today. If you think you can't sleep in my bed, then sleep on my couch and get some rest. No one will know."

"What about all those phone calls?"

"They're leaving messages. When they ask you why you didn't answer, tell them you were too upset. It'll make them feel guilty." He turned and entered his bedroom. He came back with a sheet, a blanket, a pillow, and a pair of sweatpants and a T-shirt. "Here's everything you need for tonight. There's a new toothbrush in the bathroom. Toby and Elizabeth got it when they did the grocery shopping for me."

"Are you sure you don't mind?"

"It won't make me any difference at all. I'll be up and out of here early in the morning. Okay?"

She hesitated, but finally she took the clothes from him and headed to the hall bath. "And you won't tell anyone?" she asked over her shoulder.

"Not me. I told you I'm not marrying anyone here. Why would I risk my freedom just to gossip?"

She glared at him, then closed the door to the bathroom.

JON GRINNED to himself after she'd closed the door. She was a cute little thing. He couldn't believe he was thinking about her that way, but he was. He'd been thrown by her coloring and size when he'd first met her, but now that he was coming to know her, he was able to appreciate her feminine charms.

He started cleaning off the table while he grinned even more. She wouldn't react favorably if he told her that. She was spoiling for a fight because she thought she'd seemed weak. He couldn't imagine tolerating all the hassle of today when she was still grieving.

She was close to Russ, and he knew she liked Abby, too. According to what he'd seen and heard the past few days, the entire family had loved Abby. But Tori had been patient and kind to everyone who called or came by, as far as he knew. He was glad he'd thought to check on her when he left the clinic.

In fact, he'd enjoyed the evening, taking care of Tori. He was glad her family was going to be there tomorrow. It wouldn't be good for the town to think he was taking care of her. Or, as she said, they'd have him married to her in their heads.

The bathroom door opened and Tori came out. He stood and stared.

She hadn't put on the pants. Her bare legs were great-looking, well-defined muscles, smooth skin. The T-shirt came to the top of her knees, but he'd only seen her in pants. When he realized she hadn't said anything, he snapped his gaze from her legs.

"Uh, will that work okay?" he asked. His T-shirt shoulder seams came to her elbows.

"I didn't use the pants. I was afraid they'd be too hot and—and the T-shirt is as long as a dress."

He cleared his throat. Thinking about her curvaceous body beneath that soft T-shirt and nothing else made it hard to look away. He wanted to slide his hands up under the T-shirt so he could stroke her skin.

"Jon? I mean, Dr. Wilson!"

"I think we'd better make it Jon. Roommates shouldn't be formal." His gaze fastened on her breasts pushing against the material.

"We're not roommates! I mean, temporarily, just for tonight. It doesn't count."

"Right," he agreed, forcing himself to look away. "Uh, it's early. You want to watch TV for a while?" He couldn't think of anything else they could do, except maybe make love. *Don't think that!* he warned himself.

She looked around the room. "I don't see a TV."

"Uh, it's in my bedroom. I usually lie on the bed and watch it."

She looked at the door that led to his bedroom, then at him. "I don't think that's a good idea. I mean, I don't want to—to crowd you."

"You won't. It's a big bed. And *NYPD Blue* is on. It's one of my favorite shows."

"Mine, too, but—"

"Then come on. I'll behave," he assured her with

a grin. Leading the way into his bedroom, he added, "Better grab the pillow off the couch."

When the show began, she was way on the other side of the bed, sitting upright, watching the television. Jon watched the show…and her. After ten minutes, she kept closing her eyes and then jerking awake. Another ten minutes, she was curled up, sound asleep. And the T-shirt hem had worked its way to her thighs.

She must have been exhausted from the emotional strain.

She was the biggest temptation he'd faced since the sixth grade, when he'd peeped down a girl's dress though he knew he shouldn't.

When the show was over, he rolled out of bed on his side and came around the bed, staring at Tori. Then he hurried into the living room to spread out the bedding. He brought his own pillow out because he couldn't move the one she was sleeping on.

With a sigh of half pleasure, half pain, he rounded the bed and slid his arms underneath her knees and her shoulders. She gasped and he figured she'd woken up. He started to speak, but she settled against him, moaning softly.

Mercy. She hadn't woken up. Her forehead rested against his neck. Her warm breath fell on his chin. Her hand rested against his chest.

He wanted to put her back in his bed. To cuddle her against him all night. Just cuddle. He wouldn't take advantage of her. But he figured she'd count that a betrayal. With a sigh, he carried her into the living room and placed her head on his pillow. Then, regretfully, he covered her up.

It took him a long time to go to sleep that night.

TORI WAS UNLOCKING the office door when her family arrived the next morning. In addition to her mother and sister, her father greeted her.

After throwing her arms around his neck in welcome, she asked, "What are you doing here, Dad?"

"I thought I might be able to do some of Russ's work, since he's using my software."

"Do you have time?" Tori asked.

"I can manage a day or two. Don't want you to get too far behind."

"You're the best!" she told him, trying to hold back tears. "You all are. Thank you so much."

Jessica grinned. "Like I had a choice. Mom was all ready with the chicken pox story."

"Don't listen to her, Tori. She agreed at once," Anna assured her oldest.

Jessica shrugged. "It will be nice to be busy. Everyone's so sad." She blinked away tears. "Sorry, but it's hard."

"I know."

"Did you stay with Jon last night?" Anna asked.

"Mom!" Tori protested just as the front door opened. She grabbed her mother by the arm and pulled her into the empty office she intended to occupy once they had a receptionist. "I don't want it announced to everyone. I slept on his couch, that's all."

"Darling, that's what I meant."

Tori sighed. She had a few questions about last night she wanted to ask Jon, but not in front of her mother or, especially, her father. It was a good thing he'd already gone into Russ's office.

Her mother looked around. "This is a nice office. Why aren't you using it?"

"I'm going to. As soon as we find a receptionist. We need someone to greet customers."

"Ah. Why don't you ask Jessica? She was fussing about not having any extra money. She spends all her allowance on clothes."

It would only be a temporary solution to their problem, but Tori was interested. She didn't think she could work alone anymore. At least for a while. And maybe by the end of the summer, they'd find someone who would take it permanently.

"That's a good idea, Mom. I'll go ask her."

Jessica was making an entry on the list Tori had started of people who'd sent plants. "Two more potted plants," she said as she wrote.

"Jess, would you be interested in working as my receptionist this summer, until you go back to school?"

"Hmm, what are you paying?"

"For you, little sister, I'll pay ten dollars an hour, but don't tell anyone else that."

Anna protested, but both girls shushed her. "It will be worth it to have someone here with me," Tori said.

"But surely Russ will be back. He can't just stop

working," Anna said. "That wouldn't be healthy for him."

"I hope not, but this going off into the woods scares me. Russ and Abby were so—so together."

"I know," Anna agreed with a sigh.

"I'LL BE BACK AT TWO, Faye. I'm taking a long lunch," Jon informed his receptionist. He didn't have any appointments until then. He thought he'd take the Randall ladies out to lunch since Anna had told him last night that she and Jessica were coming in to help Tori today.

He strode down the sidewalk, wondering if Tori was doing better today. He felt sure her mother was protecting her from the stress of yesterday.

He'd left early this morning, making clinic rounds at seven. He'd left a note for Tori and had set his alarm for eight o'clock. He'd decided it might be best to avoid her when she first awakened.

He opened the door to the accounting office and a young lady with glorious auburn hair, sitting efficiently at the desk where Tori usually was, greeted him.

"Good morning, may I help you?"

"You must be Jessica." Even as she nodded, he said, "I'm Dr. Jon Wilson. I'm sorry I didn't meet you at the funeral, but it seemed an inappropriate time for introductions. Is your sister or your mother here?"

"Is that you, Jon?" Anna's voice floated from the empty office. Then she appeared in the doorway.

"Hi, Anna. How's everything going?"

"Fine. Oh, and thanks for last night."

"No problem," Jon said, looking over Anna's shoulder for any sign of Victoria.

"Did you need some information about your account?" Anna asked.

Jon frowned. "No, I thought you might all be ready for lunch. I'm offering to treat you all. Anyone interested?"

Jessica didn't hesitate. "I'm ready!"

"That's so kind of you," Anna added. "But there's four of us today. Brett came in with us."

"Your husband? I haven't met him yet." Not a subtle hint, but it worked.

"Come in and I'll introduce you."

Not only was he going to meet Brett Randall, but he also discovered Victoria, leaning over her father's shoulder.

"Brett," Anna called. "I want you to meet the doctor—Jon Wilson—I've been talking about."

A tall, handsome, dark-haired, brown-eyed man, who looked a lot like Russ, stood and extended his hand. "Glad to meet you, Doctor," he said, a warm smile on his face.

"Please, make it Jon. Otherwise, everyone will confuse me with Doc."

"Call me Brett. Anna said you helped Tori last night. I appreciate it."

"It wasn't much. I thought I'd offer to take everyone to lunch." He paused, then added, "Hi, Tori."

"Dr. Wilson," she acknowledged, barely glancing at him.

"How about it, everyone? Shall we join Jon here for lunch?" Brett asked, looking at the women of his family. Jessica had joined them at the office door.

Jessica and Anna showed their pleasure at the idea.

Tori took a step backward. "You all go ahead. I'll stay here and keep an eye on things."

Jon frowned. "I think you should come, take a break."

"He's right, little girl," Brett said. "You carried the burden yesterday. Not today. We'll lock it up and go eat."

Though she frowned at Jon, she quietly said, "Yes, Daddy."

They all walked across the street to the café. As Jon walked with Brett, he whispered, "I'm impressed, Tori doing exactly what you said."

Brett chuckled. "Don't be. I'm worried when they do what I say. It usually means they're up to something." He looked at Jon, one eyebrow up. "You two have a fight?"

"No! Not at all."

"You just remember she's my little girl. Okay?"

"Of course."

The ladies had already gone into the café and Jon held the door for Brett. By the time they got to the table, a big round booth for six, Victoria was sitting between her sister and her mother, making sure Jon couldn't sit next to her.

A WEEK LATER, Jon stopped by the accounting office again. He'd barely seen Tori. He'd offered lunch again, but he ended up with Jessica. He'd asked her questions about her sister, but she wouldn't say much.

He wasn't sure why Tori was avoiding him. But he had a good reason for coming this afternoon. Russ had been gone a week, and he was worried about him.

Jessica looked up when he came in. "Hi, Jon. It's a little late for lunch."

"Yeah, it is. Is Victoria in?"

"Yes, but she's working."

"So am I. Please tell her I need to see her about Russ."

Jessica frowned but picked up the phone and punched in two numbers. She repeated his words into the phone. Then she hung up the receiver. Before she could say anything, the door on the left opened and Victoria stared at him.

"Come in, Dr. Wilson."

His gaze swallowed her whole. Her face looked pale and she had shadows under her eyes. He wanted to wrap her in his arms and promise to take care of her.

He walked into the office. The last time he'd seen it, it had been empty. Now there was a rug on the floor, a large desk with a computer and several wing chairs in front of the desk. "You furnished the office. It's nice. Is that why you're so tired?"

"I thought you had questions about Russ."

"I do. I was just making conversation first. Trying to be polite." He could tell she wasn't buying that excuse.

Putting the desk between them, she sat down after

waving him to a wing chair. "What do you want to know?"

"Has Russ been heard from?"

She looked away. "No. He hasn't."

"Is someone going to go check on him?"

"Uncle Pete says no. He said he promised Russ that no one would bother him."

"I think he's been out there by himself long enough."

She leaned forward with a sigh. "I know. I'm worried about him, but I'm not sure what to do."

"Could you draw a map to this place?"

"What? Why?"

"Why? Because I want to go see him."

"Doctors don't make house calls. Did you forget?"

"And you didn't even crack a smile." He studied her face. "What's wrong, Tori? I thought we were becoming friends last week." He watched her closely. He'd been wanting to ask that question for a long time.

"I don't know what you're talking about."

"At one time you called me Jon. Now we're back to Dr. Wilson. Why?"

"I'm trying to keep the town from thinking there's anything between us." She glared at him, as if he were mentally deficient.

"Fine. You didn't answer my question."

"Which one?"

"Can you draw me a map?"

"Of course not. I can't let you go out into the wilderness on your own. You'd get lost and would never be seen again.''

"Then go with me.''

"Jon, forget it. You can't go looking for him.''

"But I'm concerned. Russ was in bad shape when he left. Without anyone to talk to, he may go off the deep end.''

"I'll talk to Uncle Pete again. That's the best I can do.''

She stood and opened the door to her office.

"Does that mean I'm supposed to leave?''

"Yes. I'm trying to finish up some work before I stop for the evening.''

"Want to have dinner with me later?'' He couldn't resist giving it another try. He didn't intend to marry anyone, but that didn't mean he couldn't enjoy female company.

"No, thank you.''

With a sigh, he walked out, saying goodbye to Jessica as he went.

TORI THOUGHT ABOUT Jon's words the rest of the day. It was difficult to go against any of the brothers. Her father and uncles were so dear. But she'd been wondering if it was wise to leave Russ out there all alone.

She decided tomorrow evening she'd go to the ranch and have dinner. Tomorrow morning, she'd call her mother and see if that would be all right. She had good reason. She'd invested in Russ's business. If the business fell through, she'd lose a lot of money.

Then she shook her head. That wasn't why she was

worried. She loved Russ, as she did all her cousins. But she and Russ were close because they were both quiet. Well, she used to be. He'd been in Rich's shadow. When he and Abby found each other, it was as if he had moved into the sunshine.

She'd lost Abby. They all had. But she wasn't going to sit back and lose Russ, too. Her mother had once told her she'd win her battles if she fought for what she wanted. She wanted Russ safe.

By Friday night, she'd made her decision. She was going to find Russ the next morning. On Thursday, she'd expressed her concern to Uncle Pete, but he'd been adamant that he'd promised his son and he was keeping his word.

Tori was pretty sure Janie, Russ's mother, wasn't in agreement with her husband, but her aunt didn't know what to do.

Well, Tori did. She was going out to the ranch and would steal a couple of horses and trek over the mountains to the cabin. The trip would take all day.

A knock on her door brought her to a halt. She checked her watch. It was almost nine o'clock. "Who is it?"

"Jon." When she didn't respond, he added, "I need to talk to you."

She stood and opened the door a few inches. "Yes?"

"What are you doing in there? Sounds like you're rearranging the furniture. Need some help?"

"No, thank you," she said coolly, and started closing the door.

He quickly stuck his foot in the way. "You never told me what you found out about Russ. Did you ask his dad?"

"Yes, and he's still convinced he should wait for Russ to come back."

"And you agree?"

She said nothing.

"Tori?"

"I'm busy, Jon. Go home."

"You're hiding something."

"How would you know? You don't know me. Leave me alone. Mind your own business."

"When are you going?"

She stared at him. He couldn't know. "What are you talking about?"

"When are you going to find Russ?"

She licked her lips and looked away. "This is none of your business."

"You didn't think I should go by myself. I don't think you should, either."

"I live here."

"I'm a doctor. Suppose you get there and he needs medical help? Wouldn't it be good if I was with you?"

"There's no reason he'd need medical help. You're just trying to scare me."

"Then why are you going to find him, if you don't think he's in trouble?"

She walked away from the door. "I think he's sad."

"Of course he's sad. Look, I just want to help.

Russ has been good to me. I want to do what I can for him. Let me go with you.''

"Have you ever been on a horse?''

"Yeah. I'm no expert, but I can ride.''

"You'll have to be ready at six-thirty in the morning. Pack one change of clothes. I'll add enough food for you. And be prepared to face Uncle Pete's wrath. I haven't told them I'm going.''

"You sound like a general,'' he said with a grin.

But she wasn't smiling. "You'd better believe it. I'm going to be in charge. If you go, you'll do what I say.''

Chapter Six

When Tori thought about Jon going with her, she was torn between relief and fear. She hadn't wanted to make the trip alone. She couldn't ask one of her male cousins to go against Pete's wishes. But she was worried about spending more time with Jon. She was attracted to him. She didn't want to admit it, but it was true.

After she'd spent the night on his sofa, she'd realized she had a problem. First of all, she didn't know how she'd gotten to the sofa. And secondly, her pillow carried his scent. She'd slept like a baby, and she'd dreamed she'd been held in Jon's arms.

Now she was taking him on an overnight trip?

But nothing would happen. Russ would be there. At least she prayed to God he was there.

She opened her door at six-thirty that morning and the sun was peeping over the horizon. If the man wasn't ready, she was leaving him there. But he was sitting in front of his door, calmly waiting.

He stood, and Tori held her breath. This was her first time to see him in tight-fitting jeans. He always wore slacks while he worked as a doctor. Now he was dressed like a cowboy, with a jacket on his arm. He held a backpack and his doctor's bag. "Okay?" he asked.

She checked out his footwear. He obviously didn't have cowboy boots, but he was wearing hiking boots. "Do you have a hat?" she asked.

"I've got a baseball cap. That's all."

"Get it. I might be able to find you a hat, but I'm not sure."

He unlocked his door and went in.

"I'm going on down," she called, but he was out of his apartment and locking the door as she finished.

"Right." He hurried down the stairs behind her. "Should we take my SUV?"

"No. My car is familiar to the family. They won't think anything about me being there. I want to get away before they investigate."

"Won't they notice the horses missing?"

"Yes, but hopefully not until tonight when they find my note. We're going to get to the ranch about the time they ride out. Once they're off to work, we'll be able to mount up without drawing any attention."

He frowned. "Look, Tori, I don't know if I can saddle a horse."

"Don't worry. I can."

After turning into the driveway a few minutes later, Tori parked the car on the crest of the hill that looked out over the Randall spread.

"Wow, this is a big place," Jon said, taking it all in.

"Yes, it's home to a lot of Randalls."

"How many still live here?" he asked.

"The four brothers, their wives, Red and Mildred, and all the kids except Rich and Sam. They live with Rich's grandmother because he manages the ranch for her. Russ and Abby had their own house. I don't know what will happen now." She paused and swallowed. "And then me and Caroline."

"Caroline?"

"My cousin. She's in med school in Chicago."

"Randall? Caroline Randall? And does she have the typical russet hair, like your sister?"

"Yes."

"I think I've met her."

Instead of answering, Tori eased her car down the driveway, going very slowly. "The men just rode out." She pulled to a halt by the second barn. "Don't slam your door."

After she chose the horses, it was Jon who placed the saddles on the horses' backs. And Tori who dealt with the buckles and the bridles. Then she chose a packhorse and belted a contraption that allowed her to load their needs onto its back. She added two bedrolls from a cabinet and covered everything with a waterproof tarp.

"You keep the bedrolls in the barn?" he asked in surprise.

"This is the indoor arena. We keep a lot of things in here. Wait here." She slipped away through another door and Jon stood there, holding the reins for the three animals. What he'd do if someone caught him, he didn't know.

When she came back, she was holding a hat. "Here, put this on."

"But it's not mine. I can't—"

"It's Dad's. Put it on." She glared at him. "Remember, I'm in charge."

He put it on.

She pulled a piece of paper out of her pocket and a pushpin. Then she tacked the paper to the last stall. "Now they won't worry when they come in tonight."

She took the reins from his hands and led the animals outside. "Mount up," she ordered, handing him the reins to the larger of the three animals. "He's well trained."

Jon swung into the saddle, not with the grace of her uncles or cousins, but he managed a credible mount.

With ease she mounted and wrapped the reins of the packhorse around her pommel. "We're going to go slow for a few minutes, until we get some distance from the house, like we're on a casual ride. Then we'll pick up speed until we get to rough country."

After that, she didn't have to worry about making conversation. She kept checking to be sure he was managing, but he was an acceptable rider, at least on level ground.

THREE HOURS LATER, Tori called a halt. They were starting to climb and she thought it was a good time for a break. Jon hadn't slowed her down, which had surprised her.

"What's wrong?" he asked as he pulled up beside her.

"Nothing. We're taking a break."

"I can go on," he assured her, frowning.

"And you will. Right now we're taking a break. There's water here for the horses, and some grass, too. You have to take care of your ride."

"Oh. Right."

She led the horses to the edge of a small creek. As they drank their fill, she took out a thermos, a plastic cup, and a pack of oatmeal-raisin cookies. She handed all that to Jon and led the horses over to a grassy area. She dropped the reins to the ground and came back toward Jon.

"Aren't you going to tie them up?"

"No. They're fine."

She sat down on the grass and stretched her arms up for the things she'd handed him. He gave them to her but remained standing.

"Aren't you going to sit down?"

He gave her a rueful grin. "I'm afraid if I do, I won't be able to get up again. It's been a while since I've ridden."

She admired his honesty. A lot of men refused to admit a weakness. "I'll help you up. I promise I won't leave you behind. And if you stretch out a little, it will hurt less this evening.

"Okay, I'll give it a try." With a few moans, he managed to get down.

Tori handed him the plastic cup filled with steaming coffee.

"What are you going to use?"

"The top of the thermos." Then she opened the pack of cookies. "These are as close to breakfast as I could figure out. They're oatmeal-raisin cookies. Think of it as oatmeal."

"Thanks. I didn't eat much breakfast." He ate several cookies before he spoke again. "The cookies are great."

"Eat as many as you want. I've got more for the morning."

"When we start back?"

She nodded.

"Okay."

She grinned. "You don't sound as enthusiastic as you were earlier."

"I know. But I won't quit."

"Good. Now stand up, if you're through eating cookies."

He grabbed a couple more in his hands and struggled to stand. He made it and sighed. "We mount up again?"

"Not yet. Stretch your legs. It will help."

He followed her instructions, then asked, "You got a pillow for my saddle?"

"Nope. You're on your own, there, cowboy."

JON FOLLOWED in the tracks of his own personal cowgirl. He'd thought she looked so cute this morning in her jeans, boots and cowboy hat. Like a little girl playing dress-up. But she was comfortable in her clothes, and she'd demonstrated her skills all morning.

The way she swung back into the saddle showed her endurance, too. He clambered on like the greenest dude in the world. Damn, he was sore! She'd said it was a nine- or ten-hour ride, so he only had six or seven more hours.

He shifted in the saddle. He focused on Victoria's trim behind. Maybe her sexy appearance could distract him from his woes. It didn't take long for him to discover that an arousal in tight jeans on the back of a horse was a big mistake.

As they rode upward on narrow trails, he appreciated his horse even more than when they started. He was a surefooted animal. "Hey, what's this horse's name?"

She looked over her shoulder. "I didn't think I should tell you until you'd spent some time on his back."

"Why?" he asked suspiciously.

"His name is Devil."

Jon stared at her in confusion. "Why? He's well behaved." He feared the horse had a trick he hadn't played yet, like throwing him off on the steepest trail.

"Don't worry. Casey, my youngest cousin, got to name him and he thought he looked like Red's devil's food cake. But if I'd told you that this morning, you probably wouldn't have believed me."

"You're right. What's your horse's name?"

"Snowflake. The packhorse is Snoopy. Now we're all introduced."

"Yeah."

"We're going to stop for lunch when we get to the top of this ridge. Can you hang on that long?"

His cheeks flushed. She must have seen how desperate he was for a distraction. "You bet," he returned, trying to sound enthusiastic. Then he ground his teeth and closed his eyes, trusting Devil to follow Snowflake and Snoopy to the top. Sounded as if he was in a damn fairy tale instead of a torture chamber.

TORI LEANED against a tree and watched Jon sleeping. They'd stopped for lunch. After he wolfed down the roast beef sandwiches, she'd suggested he lie down for a few minutes. She'd told him to use his jacket as a pillow. After he'd done so, she spread her jacket over his chest.

Riding all day required seasoning, just as a runner didn't start with a marathon. This was going to be a hard trip for the doctor. He was going way beyond the care most doctors offered. She didn't want to admire the man…but she did. And if they got there to find Russ in trouble, she'd be even more grateful.

When she got back to town, it was going to be impossible to return to the formality she'd tried to cling to. She'd better line up some women to introduce to the doctor. The brothers had intended to have a big party on the Fourth of July to celebrate the holiday, and the twins' birthday and anniversary. Rich and Russ had both married in a joint ceremony last year.

She didn't know what they would do now.

If Russ was all right, they might go ahead with it. It was a tradition to have a July Fourth party. It all depended on Russ. Poor Rich and Samantha were expecting their first child in three months. Janie said Rich was watching Samantha like a hawk. They were sharing the house with his grandmother, and Rich was grateful for someone to be at home with Samantha all day.

Toby had muttered something about not having another child. They had a baby boy born last November. He'd talked of having a houseful of children, but after Abby's death, he'd changed his mind.

A gentle snore interrupted her thoughts. She looked at Jon. He seemed to be a good doctor. Maybe he could reassure Rich and Toby. Toby's boy was going to be spoiled rotten if some more babies didn't come along fast. Of course, Samantha was due in three months. A little girl.

Samantha was so excited. She'd had a difficult life until she met Rich. And Janie, Rich's mother, was over the moon about a baby girl. She'd had three boys and wanted grandchildren, especially girls.

Which only reminded Tori of the loss of Abby and her unborn child. Life could be unbelievably cruel. The family had been fortunate for a long time.

She checked her watch. It had been half an hour. That was as long as she could give him. She stood and crossed to the grassy area where he was sleeping.

He looked so young, lying there sprawled on the grass. The recurring dream of him holding her in his arms, which had bothered her since she'd spent the night at his apartment, flashed through her mind.

Better not think of that. She bent down and shook his shoulder. "Jon? Time to go."

He rubbed his eyes and stared up at her. "Oh, yeah."

He groaned as he sat up. "Did I go to sleep?"

"I don't know," she said with a grin. "Does snoring count?"

His cheeks flushed. "Oh, sorry."

She wanted to hug him. He was so different from the stiff doctor she'd first met in her office. Instead, she offered him a hand up.

"Thanks," he said as he stood, adding a small moan. "Did you get any rest?"

"No, but I'm more used to riding. Only about five hours left. We'll take another break in a few hours. I brought along another snack."

"I think I could eat anything right now, let alone in three hours. I can't believe my appetite."

"Mountain air. You might want to put on your jacket. There's a breeze picking up and we're higher up."

"Is there going to be a storm?"

She frowned and stared to the west. "I'm not as good at knowing these things as Red, but I think it's a possibility. Hopefully rain and not snow."

"You're kidding!"

She laughed at his amazement. "You're going to be here four years. You'll see."

They mounted up, Jon with some difficulty, and they were on the trail again. A snack in two or three hours. Maybe that would keep him going.

TWO HOURS LATER, the storm had come. Rain was pouring down and Jon realized why she'd told him to wear the cowboy hat. His baseball cap would have protected his face, but it would have left his neck bare, with rain pouring inside his jacket.

Trees were not as thick, so they must be getting closer to the tree line, where it was too high for them to grow. At least it made the paths a little wider. When they came across another tree ahead offering a little shelter from the rain, Victoria stopped her horse under its branches.

"I don't think we should dismount, but maybe we'll wait here a few minutes and see if the rain stops. Want your snack now?"

He growled. "I think I could eat Snoopy at the moment."

"Don't say that. He'll run away with the snack."

"My apologies, Snoopy. I didn't realize you were so sensitive."

She gave him a sympathetic smile. "I'm going to share my addiction with you, but you mustn't tell anyone."

"I hope your addiction is for T-bone steaks."

When he looked hopefully at her, she giggled. "Nope, afraid not. I'm addicted to cupcakes. The ones with cream in the center.'' She pulled out a package of cellophane-wrapped cupcakes.

He looked at the two cupcakes in his package and figured they'd last him about two seconds. But they were better than nothing. Ripping off the packaging, which he slipped into his jacket pocket, he practically swallowed them whole. But he found them surprisingly satisfying.

''I think it's all the chocolate, but they always pick me up, don't you think?'' Tori asked him.

''Yeah. You wouldn't happen to have any more, would you?''

She offered another package, much to his surprise. ''I was actually joking,'' he admitted. ''I'll split them with you.''

She grinned. ''I have another package, too. This is a hard trip. It takes a lot of energy, even for an experienced rider. You're doing very well, but we still have a couple of hours to go.''

They munched in silence, listening to the raindrops hitting the leaves overhead. It was an amazingly peaceful place.

Until a bolt of lightning ripped the sky.

''Ooh! We've got to get away from the tree. So I guess we'd better go ahead. Hopefully we'll ride out of the storm soon.''

Jon could only agree.

While he wouldn't recommend four cupcakes as a snack, he agreed with Victoria. They had an amazing effect on him. It had to be the chocolate. He'd have to remember to put them on his shopping list if he ever planned a trip into the mountains again. Especially if Tori accompanied him.

He'd watched her tongue dig into the cream center, pleasure in her eyes. It hadn't taken a second to want to see that look on her face again, her tongue seeking something else. In spite of his aches and pains, he was finding this ride amazingly pleasurable.

The trail took a dip into a small valley. Jon preferred riding up to riding down, though he had no choice but to follow Victoria. At least the rain wasn't in his face so much with his head down.

It was easy to pretend it was a hundred years earlier and he was a man heading west to build his life with his woman, his wife. The courage of the pioneers had been remarkable. That thought gave him something to think about besides Tori.

When they reached the bottom, Tori pulled up and waited for him to reach her side. "I just wanted you to know that the cabin sits on the top of this ridge. It's only half as high as the one we just crossed. We'll be there in about an hour, then we'll be able to get out of the rain. Are you soaked?"

He nodded. "Pretty much, but thanks for the encouragement."

With a nod, she started off again.

One hour. He could last that long, surely. Even though his legs were aching, his rear was sore, his— well, everything below the waist was in pain, he could last one more hour. Too bad Tori didn't offer him any more cupcakes. Eating seemed to dull the pain.

The rain was a little lighter as they rode, but the

nearby trees were shedding their water, so they were still getting just as wet. Jon wished for the warm sunshine back in Rawhide. Back in civilization. Then he chuckled to himself. He'd considered Chicago to be civilization when he'd first arrived.

But beggars couldn't be choosers.

WHEN THE CABIN CAME into sight, Tori's heart beat faster. She had thought she remembered the way, but she was afraid she'd miss it, especially in the rain. Of course, she hadn't told Jon that.

Then she noticed there was no smoke coming out of the chimney. It was a chilly day up here in the high country, especially with the rainstorm. There were no lights in the cabin, either. Kerosene lights. That's what they used up here. Maybe Russ had fallen asleep and didn't realize it was so dark.

Forgetting about Jon, she spurred her horse forward, picking up the pace for the first time in hours. Her anxiety about Russ was greater than ever.

She could hear Jon coming faster, too. Still, it took several minutes to cover the distance. She pulled Snowflake to a halt and swung out of the saddle. "Russ? Russ? Where are you?"

The door didn't open. Silence was the only response.

She tied the reins to the hitching post and ran up the wooden steps, out of the rain. The door was unlocked and she shoved it open and stepped inside.

Nothing moved. He wasn't here.

She turned to go back out and ran into Jon.

"He's not here."

"Maybe he went out for the day and hasn't come back yet," he suggested, his voice hopeful.

She rushed around him.

"Where are you going?"

"To see if his horse is still here."

His favorite horse was in the repaired corral. There was grass growing inside the corral and a water barrel, so a horse could manage for quite a while without a man to feed him.

She walked slowly back to the cabin, wondering if Jon could be right and Russ would come back in a while.

Or was he gone forever, like Abby.

Chapter Seven

Jon moved to the porch of the old cabin and waited for Tori. He was glad to be out of the rain, but he shared Tori's concern about Russ.

She rounded the cabin, her head down.

"Is the horse there?"

Her head snapped up, as if she'd forgotten his presence. "Oh, yes. The horse is there."

"So maybe he went for a walk, Tori. It's not like he knew we were coming."

"Yes, of course. I'm going to unstrap the saddles. Can you lift them off and put them on the porch? Then I'll take the horses to the corral."

"Won't they need food and water?"

"There's grass growing in the corral and a water barrel that was filled today from the rainstorm."

They unsaddled the horses without comment. When Jon offered to take the horses to the corral, she refused, asking him to carry all their supplies inside. "Otherwise, we'll awake to a family of bears treating themselves."

He piled their supplies on the big table that seated

eight in the middle of the kitchen part of the cabin. There were also four sets of bunk beds against the walls in the living area with a fireplace in the middle, and that was all the furniture. He'd noted the wood piled on the porch and brought some in to start a fire. By the time Tori came inside, he'd started a small fire.

She glanced at it as she shrugged off her wet jacket. "Thanks." Then she looked in a corner and brought out an old-fashioned laundry rack. She spread her jacket out and told him to do the same to his. "We don't want to start out wet in the morning."

He couldn't agree more. "Is there anywhere in particular you used to visit when you came up here?"

"There's a lovely view at one place. The guys used to call it—" she paused and caught her breath "—Lover's Leap. You don't think—I can't believe—no!" She turned away and moved to the kitchen area, taking down two glass lamps. She reached under the sink to pull out a can of kerosene and filled both lamps.

After lighting the first, she set it on the window ledge over the sink. The other she carried to the mantel over the fireplace.

Without speaking, she stood staring down into the fire.

"Is it very far?" he asked quietly.

"I—I don't know. It's been a long time—we'll have to wait until morning." Her voice sounded leaden, heavy.

"He may be back before then," was the best Jon

could offer. He didn't know Russ well enough to guess what he might have done.

She walked back over to the table and began digging into the supplies.

"Looking for something?" he asked.

"Dinner. I'll have it ready in about fifteen minutes."

"Do you think Russ did any cooking?" Jon asked. "There's a pile of dirty clothes over here and his sleeping bag on this lower bunk, but either he's very neat or he hasn't been preparing much food." Jon moved closer to Victoria, waiting for her answer.

"Whatever he did, he's almost out of supplies." She pulled four big cans of stew out of their pack and set them on the table. "Good thing I brought plenty. We may be here for several days."

He'd figured as much. He guessed Tori didn't intend to go back home without Russ, if possible. By the time they found Lover's Leap and climbed down and back up again, half the day would be gone.

They couldn't start back then, or if they did they'd have to camp overnight on the trail. "Anything I can do to help?"

"No, thank you."

There was a small potbellied stove in the kitchen for cooking and Tori quickly built a fire in it and poured the cans of stew into a big pot, putting it on the top of the stove. Then she mixed batter for biscuits and baked several of them in a Dutch oven. In a few minutes the smell of beef stew, even canned, and baking bread only increased the hunger Jon was feeling.

When she filled two bowls and set the bread on the table, she didn't have to call him to dinner. He was standing beside the table, waiting.

After he sat down, she walked to the door and opened it, looking out into the night.

"Did you hear something?" he asked, not sure if he should join her or not.

"No. I just thought—it's already dark." She closed the door and came back to the table.

He waited until she picked up her own spoon before he started eating. He didn't look up again until his bowl was empty, "That was great," he told Tori, feeling he'd been greedy.

She barely smiled, then reached into a sack. "These are our only desserts." She slid out onto the table two packets of cupcakes. "Sorry there isn't more."

He lifted her hand to his lips. "You've provided great food, honey. You've handled everything, in fact. Thanks for taking care of me."

She jumped up from the table, mumbling "You're welcome" and grabbing her bowl and spoon and putting them in the sink. Jon instantly followed, not wanting her to think he expected her to clean up without him. "Why don't you sit down and rest and I'll wash up."

"No!" Even she seemed surprised by the snap in her voice. "I—I have to have something to do."

"You wash, I'll dry," he suggested softly, understanding her discomfort.

They did the dishes in silence, until Jon asked, "How often have you come up here?"

"Every summer," she said after a silence. "It became a dad-and-kids trip. The moms stayed on the ranch and the brothers let all the kids ten and up come on the ride. I was so excited the first trip. And scared. I wanted Dad to be proud of me. And I thought it was so great that Jessica didn't get to go yet." She smiled faintly. "I wish she were here now."

He watched her out of the corner of his eye. "You two don't seem much alike."

"No. I don't look like any of them. Mom says I look like her mother. I began to wonder if I was really a Randall, but Mom says there's no doubt of that."

Jon chuckled. "She's right. You've got that stubborn determination, that sense of right and wrong and the willingness to do for others. From what I've seen, those are all Randall traits."

She looked at him in surprise. "Do you think so?"

"Yeah, I do. You and Russ are close, aren't you?"

She closed her eyes and he saw a tear slip past her guard and trail down her cheek and he could have kicked himself.

But she answered almost at once. She nodded and said, "He always seemed to be in Rich's shadow. I never felt like I fit in, either, and he helped me out a lot. But all my cousins are like brothers and sisters. We may fuss and fight among ourselves, especially the boys, but no one criticizes one of us, without having to face us all backing each other.

"That's why I had to come find Russ. He needs us

now. He needs—'' She broke off in a sob. ''We need to hold tight, to get through our sorrow.''

He put down the towel and put his arms around Tori. She didn't come to his shoulder, but he didn't for a minute think of her as a child. What he felt for Tori had nothing to do with children.

''Hold on, Tori. We're going to find Russ. It's going to be all right.'' He stroked her back soothingly, praying he was right. She pressed against him, burying her face against his chest.

''I can't stand it, Jon. It hurts so much.''

He didn't know if she meant Russ or Abby, but he felt her pain and sympathized with her, and he wasn't even family. ''We'll get through this, Tori, we will.'' He kissed her forehead, the top of her head, and pressed her tighter against him, wanting to do anything to please her, to distract her.

She lifted her head and tried to smile, to thank him for his comfort, and his lips covered hers. Gently he caressed her, his mouth leaving hers to press gentle kisses on her face, but it kept coming back to her soft lips.

When her arms went around his neck, lifting her breasts against his chest, it was as if lightning raked his skin, leaving heat in tender trails on his skin.

He lifted her, bringing her mouth even with his and the kissing smoldered, melting his bones and making him hungry for more, more touching, more heat. He crossed the room to the first bunk and lay her down on the thin mattress and joined her, only leaving her lips alone briefly.

His lips trailed to her slender neck. The taste of her skin was like honey, but he returned to her lips. When she responded to his searching tongue, he lifted her against his chest, allowing him to get even closer.

But it wasn't all physical. He'd first doubted her willingness to go the extra mile. He now knew her heart was the biggest part of her. She'd done everything possible for Russ. She'd mourned for Abby, too, yet she'd kept her composure and done her job.

She'd taken a long trip on horseback to save her cousin's life, and brought Jon along, too. Her care was evident in everything she did.

Her heart was an aphrodisiac, urging him to draw closer, more deeply, into her life. Even now, with her in his arms, stirring his senses, her spirit was entwined around his heart. It was too soon, of course, to think of commitment. And they still had the issue of his departure, but he wanted more. He wanted Tori.

Tori's right hand began stroking his chest. Then she pulled his shirttail out of his jeans and slid her hand under his shirt, flesh to flesh, and his skin shimmered with desire. He wanted her to touch him all over. He wanted to touch her.

When she made no resistance, he started on her shirt buttons and then got rid of her bra. The silken softness of her breasts almost had him losing control. He didn't remember when a woman had so turned him on.

"More, Jon. Touch me more," she whispered, shoving his shirt off him. He decided to help her by unzipping his jeans and shoving them down until his boots impeded his actions. "Damn, my boots," he complained, and started to sit up, but Tori, with her arms wrapped around his chest, clung to him, and separating from her was more than he could do.

He felt his entire body bathed in her warmth, her scent, her loving. She wasn't large enough to match him inch for inch, but the only part of him that lived was what she touched. He kissed her as if he would devour her, and she returned the favor. He could scarcely breathe, but that didn't matter. He needed Tori. When they were finally naked, there was no way he could hold back.

For the first time, he felt the true sense of what being one with a woman meant. He'd made love before, but he'd never felt a part of his partner, a togetherness that would never end. A mixing of emotions that would bind them together. On the outer edge of his mind, he recognized fear. But it wasn't enough to block the path he was rushing down.

When he felt her explode with passion and completion, he joined her with relief, with celebration, with completion. An incredible experience. Nirvana. True happiness.

He couldn't bear to put any distance between them. He trailed his fingers down her back, cupped her hips, stroking her flesh, wishing he never had to release her. Though they had a lot to work out, his mind began planning a future, a time when he could hold her close whenever he wished. When her care and concern would be focused on him. When she would turn to him for support. They'd share everything.

And, eventually, they'd share their lives with children. He imagined Tori, her flat stomach rounded with his child. Of course, he'd wait until she was ready but—he panicked, terror rising in him.

They hadn't used protection.

All the passion, the pleasure, was wiped away. He sat up abruptly.

TORI WASN'T that experienced. But she couldn't imagine ever having sex with anyone but Jon ever again. She felt connected, loved, celebrated…and exhausted. She never wanted to move from his arms.

Then he jerked upright. "Are you on the pill?" he demanded.

She automatically answered, "No." Then she stared at him, as if he'd been speaking a foreign language. Did he feel nothing? Hadn't their lovemaking meant anything? Had he simply wanted to get lucky? She hoped she hid her sob as he got out of the narrow bed and grabbed his underwear to cover himself.

She lay there on the bare mattress with no sheet to cover her and wanted to scream in his face.

"We didn't use protection!" he pointed out. "You could be pregnant. Is it the right time of the month? Do you know?"

She rolled off the mattress and grabbed the various articles of clothing she'd willingly shed not so long ago. Then, without answering, she went to the small, rough bathroom that opened off the back of the room.

"Tori? You didn't answer me," Jon called through the door.

With tears running down her cheeks, she dressed. Then she wiped her cheeks dry, drew a deep breath and entered the main part of the cabin again. Jon was dressed, pacing about the room.

"Tori—" he began.

She held up a hand to stop him. "I have no idea, and no, I'm not pregnant."

"I didn't mean—I shouldn't—how do you know?"

She didn't answer. The first man she'd shared her body with had been quite blunt about wanting her but not wanting anything permanent, like children. It broke her heart that Jon was the same way. Crossing to the potbellied stove, she took the old coffeepot, filled it with water and put it on the top burner to heat.

"It doesn't matter," she said coolly, not looking at him.

"But Tori—"

The front door opened and Russ Randall staggered into the cabin.

"RUSS!" TORI SCREAMED. She raced to his side, getting there even before Jon could catch him. "Russ, are you okay?"

"C-cold," he muttered. Then he collapsed.

"Dear God, please—" she prayed, falling to her knees beside him. He was soaked to the skin and he looked as if he'd lost a lot of weight. His skin was pale. He obviously hadn't taken care of himself as he'd grieved over Abby's death. Tori began struggling with his sodden jacket.

Without a word, Jon held him up while Tori removed the jacket. He stopped her when she started on the shirt. "I'll strip him and put him in his sleeping bag. You fix something hot for him to drink. Is there any of that stew left?"

"Yes, I saved some in case—for Russ. I'll heat it up." She hurried to do as Jon asked. She wanted to do the best for Russ right now, no matter how she felt about Dr. Jon Wilson.

"Do you think he's okay?" All she cared about right now was Russ's condition.

"I can't tell yet. Wait until we get something hot inside him and I can examine him."

She made a cup of instant coffee and brought it to Russ just as Jon got him in the sleeping bag. Jon laid him on the mattress, then helped him sit up to drink the coffee.

Tori wasn't going to let Jon give him the coffee. She knelt beside the bed and held the cup to Russ's lips. "Drink, Russ. It's coffee. It'll help you get warm."

He clasped two hands around the mug and sipped. When he'd had several drinks, she left him to Jon's attention and went back to the stove to see if the stew had heated up.

She returned several minutes later with a bowl of stew and a spoon. "Here's some stew, Russ. Open up."

"Wait, honey, and let me listen to his chest." Jon had his stethoscope pressed to Russ's chest. He frowned and Tori tensed.

"What's wrong?"

"He doesn't sound good. Labored breathing. I think he's running a high fever," Jon whispered. "Can you hold him and feed him at the same time? I need to get some medicine out of my bag."

She did as he asked, but she kept her eyes on Jon also. Here was the part where Jon would earn his merit badge. She had brought him here for his medical skills, not his value as a lover. She was going to forget what had happened.

With that idea in mind, she spooned some of the stew into Russ's mouth even as she watched Jon.

Russ didn't even appear to be awake, but he swallowed the liquid. So she gave him another spoonful.

In the meantime, Jon took his temperature.

She looked at him, a silent demand for information.

"One hundred four."

"Maybe part of it is the stew being hot."

Jon shook his head. "I took it in his ear, not his mouth." He pulled out his stethoscope and listened to Russ's chest again. "I don't like the way he sounds. I think he may have contracted pneumonia. I'll give him something for his fever and some antibiotics. By the time we get him home, maybe he'll be better."

Tori stared at him. "He won't be able to sit on a horse. How are we going to get him home?"

"Would Devil be able to hold both of us? I could try to hold him in the saddle."

"No, I don't think so. I'll figure out something. Can he have anything but the liquid from the stew?"

"Yes, but keep it in small pieces. We don't want him choking."

"He's still shivering. Bring my sleeping bag over here."

There were a couple of blankets she could use. It wouldn't be as comfortable, but she wanted Russ's fever broken.

After Jon had followed her orders, he stood looking at Russ. "I'm going to give him the aspirin now. Then I want you to stop feeding him for half an hour. We'll try again then. He probably hasn't eaten since yesterday."

Tori did as he said. After all, he was the medical expert. But that left her with nothing to do. She certainly wasn't going to talk to Jon about what had happened before Russ had arrived. She had no reading material and no television.

She walked around the room, unsure what to do.

"We never got around to eating our desserts," Jon reminded her. He picked up one of the packages and tossed it to Tori. She put it back on the table. "I'm saving mine for Russ. He likes them."

"Then we'll share mine."

"No, thank you."

Jon stood there holding the package of cupcakes, staring at her. "I said the wrong thing."

She ignored him.

"Tori, I was shocked that I would be so irresponsible. I shouldn't have—it was great, but—"

She spun around and glared at him. "If you are talking about what happened before Russ came back,

I do not want to discuss it ever again. We will forget it ever happened!'' Then she turned her back to him.

"Honey, I know I didn't handle—Tori, we can't just forget about it. You may be pregnant!''

"Hush! Russ might hear you!'' She grabbed her jacket off the drying rack and put it on.

"Where are you going?''

"Outside on the porch. I need some fresh air! And don't come after me! I've had enough of you, Dr. Wilson!'' She slammed the door behind her.

Once she was outside, alone in the dark, she let her defenses down. The tears that had been trying to claw their way out of her eyes did so now.

She'd never found sex too appealing. She'd thought that, as she was different from other Randalls in her looks, so too did she have differing opinions about sex. She knew boys liked it, but it seemed several of her girl cousins found it incredible. She never had.

Now, *now,* she finally discovered what everyone was talking about. She had found a man who made her feel loved, complete, perfect, and he just wanted to get lucky. All he wanted was to be sure he didn't have to pay for his fun! Oh, no, never. If paying for his fun meant having to be responsible for *her* child, he didn't have to worry.

She'd rather be a single mother, raising her child alone, than try to live with a man who didn't want her, in Chicago of all places.

No, he didn't have to worry. She didn't think she was pregnant anyway, but whether she was or not, she wasn't going to have anything to do with Jon Wilson.

If only she could stop crying.

JON DIDN'T GO OUTSIDE. He feared Tori would run off into the forest if he came out. But he had to talk to her. He had to explain everything. If he knew what everything was. He knew he should not have reacted so quickly, so alarmed, about no protection. He should have explained that his anger was with himself, not her.

He knew he was the responsible one. He was the one who'd said he wouldn't be staying in Rawhide, that he had no intention of getting involved with anyone. He was returning to Chicago. His father and great-aunt were there, alone. His mother had died. She'd been selfish and demanding, but his father had loved her.

He'd also worked very hard to help Jon with medical school. He owed his father everything. He was going back to Chicago.

But if Tori had a child, he'd certainly marry her and take them both back to Chicago with him. Chicago was a good city for children. There were the beaches, all the parks, museums and theaters. He'd convince Tori. It wouldn't be a disaster.

In fact, he'd be very happy in Chicago with Tori. The sex had been—incredible. And he wanted a family.

Yeah, everything would be all right. He'd talk to Tori and explain everything. Surely she knew he'd been stunned by the pleasure of their loving. She couldn't think he hadn't. And he was a responsible man. He'd even explain to her father.

Everything was going to be fine.

He fed Russ some more stew, because Tori hadn't come back in.

Then he paced the floor, waiting for her.

Finally he opened the door. "Tori, aren't you coming in? It's cold out there."

"Go away."

"Russ was asking for you." He figured the lie was justified, because she was going to get sick if she didn't come back in. And then what would he do?

As she came into the cabin, he asked, "So you think we have enough food to stay here until Russ is better?"

"No. We're leaving in the morning."

Chapter Eight

Jon heard Tori when she first stirred the next morning. Though there was a hint of light in the east, it was at least half an hour before the sun would show itself.

Had she, like him, not slept well? He'd tried to get her to take his sleeping bag, leaving him with those blankets, but she had stiffly refused. They were still in a cold war, and he didn't see any relief in sight. He just hoped she'd let him follow her off the mountain.

Even more he wished they had a way to contact the ranch. But before they'd made love, she'd explained that a cell phone wouldn't work up in the mountains. He would have been thrilled to have a helicopter pick them up, but there was nowhere to land. So he was stuck with a ride back down. And somehow they had to get Russ down the mountain, too.

Tori had gone into the bathroom to dress. Now the door opened and she slipped back into the main room.

"Tori? What can I do to help?"

"Nothing," she whispered tersely. Then she picked

up an ax, its blade gleaming in the limited light. Just
for a second he wondered if he should take cover,
then sanity returned. He watched her gather up some
rope and then go outside.

He got out of his sleeping bag and grabbed his
jeans. Whatever she was going to do, he needed to
be there. That ax looked lethal.

He had tried to talk to her last night about staying
another day, but she refused to discuss anything except to ask if it would hurt Russ if she could get him
down the mountain flat on his back.

He wasn't sure how she was going to do that.

He checked Russ again before he went out. He'd
gotten up at two and at six to do the same thing and
given him water and another pill. But it wasn't time
yet for his next one.

Outside, he couldn't see Tori. Suddenly he heard
the sound of metal meeting wood and he moved to
the side of the porch. He could see movement near a
stand of aspen. Tori was chopping at the base of a
young aspen, almost twelve feet tall.

He waited until the ax met the wood again. Then
he interrupted. "I'll do that."

She glared at him, but, to his surprise, she nodded
and handed the ax to him. Then, while he chopped
the tree down, she looked around the area. When the
tree fell, giving him an urge to shout "Timber," she
pointed out another tree about the same size. "That
one, too."

"Okay. Er, how many are we going to cut?"

"Just two."

When he moved to the second tree, she dragged the first one to a clear area next to the porch. When he brought the second one over, she'd tied a rope about six feet from the top. "Cut the small end off so it's about ten feet long," she ordered.

Jon watched as she zigzagged the rope from pole to pole, wrapping the rope around twice. When she'd finished, she had a rope frame. "I'm going to tie Russ and one of the mattresses to this frame, with it tied between two horses."

"That's brilliant, Tori."

Just then, raindrops began falling. She grabbed the ax and got under the porch roof. "We need to get out of here as soon as possible. Do you have a T-shirt Russ can borrow?"

"Sure."

"If you'll put that on him, I'll gather what we need to take with us. When will he need to take medicine?"

"At ten."

"Okay. Get him to the bathroom. Then make some instant coffee while I bring the horses up here to the porch. We'll want to load Russ last."

She hurried outside and he couldn't help but grin. She sounded like a no-nonsense general this morning. But she was taking the most difficult work herself. He made the coffee first. Then he unzipped Russ's sleeping bag and put a T-shirt on him. After that, he walked Russ to the bathroom. Then he sat him at the table with his coffee cup and a blanket around him.

He scattered the coals in the fireplace, rolled his

sleeping bag and stowed the last of the supplies in the satchels that had carried them. He had one empty satchel, into which he put Russ's boots. Then he stuffed their dirty clothes into a trash bag. He looked around to be sure everything was tidy.

Tori came in, solemn and intense. He wanted to kiss her, ask if everything was all right, but he didn't dare get near her. Instead, he silently handed her a coffee mug.

"The cookies are—"

"I have them here, but I didn't know if you wanted any now."

"Yes. Russ, how are you doing?"

"Fine," he mumbled, not raising his head.

"Take some cookies, but be sure to chew them. There are raisins and pecans in them. We don't want you to choke."

She picked up the neatly folded tarp. "Thank you for packing. Can you come help me saddle up?"

He slid into his warm coat, grateful they'd dried the outerwear last night. Outside, he threw the saddle on Snowflake and then Devil, Tori securing them on the horses. He put the pack carrier on Snoopy. "What do we do about Russ's horse?"

"Go ahead and put Russ's saddle on him. He's coming, too, of course." After she secured the bridle on Russ's horse, she tied the reins together and looped them over the saddle horn. "Come hold him while I load him."

"Won't he stay, like the others?"

"Not when the reins aren't on the ground, so don't let go."

He watched as she tied the end of the stretcher she'd made on each side of the saddle.

Then she did the same to Snoopy, leaving his reins on the ground. Now that Russ's horse was held by the stretcher and Snoopy, he wouldn't leave.

Then they loaded the supplies onto Snoopy and Russ's bag of dirty clothes and even his Stetson onto his horse. "By the way, this is Jack. He's Russ's favorite."

"I put Russ's boots in one of the satchels."

"Good. Let's go get Russ."

They found Russ wandering aimlessly around the big room. "I can't find my jeans," he complained, clutching the blanket around him.

"We packed them. You're traveling in a sleeping bag," Tori said matter-of-factly, as if that were normal.

Russ looked confused and started his search again.

Jon threw an arm around him. "Come on, Russ. You need to lie down again. Did you eat any cookies? They're good."

Tori looked at the table as Jon helped Russ back into his sleeping bag. "He took one bite and hardly drank any coffee. I'm going to give him some water to keep with him. I'll leave the cookies with him, too."

She did a visual sweep of the cabin, her hands on her hips, before she nodded. "Okay, let's load him."

"You take his feet. I've got his shoulders," Jon

said softly, hoping to get things under way before Russ realized what was happening.

It only took a minute to get him and his mattress out the door and onto the litter. It was still raining, but Tori had carried the tarp under her arm. She quickly spread it out over Russ, even covering his head.

The she gathered up the rope and zigzagged it over her cousin from his chest to his knees, including the mattress, so that he was firmly tied to the litter.

Jon marveled. He probably wouldn't have thought of that, but as rugged as the land was, he knew it was necessary. "His head—" He stopped as he watched Victoria pull the tarp back. Then she grabbed a pillow from the porch that he hadn't even noticed and slid it beneath Russ's head. She pulled out the flap of the bedroll and stuck two sticks through the eyelets at the end of it to make a porch effect on the litter that shielded him from the rain or the sun but allowed him to see.

Without thinking, Jon leaned over and brushed Tori's lips with his. "You're brilliant, Tori!"

"Don't touch me!"

She went back inside without waiting for his response. She immediately returned with two small canteens and plastic bags of cookies. "Here's your water and cookies."

Then she tucked her canteen and cookies into Russ's sleeping bag. "Russ, here's your water and some more cookies. Try to eat a little."

"Where's your water?" Jon asked sharply.

"I have a bottle of water and cookies in my coat pocket. Okay, I think we're ready. I'll go first, leading Snoopy. You'll come last. Your job is to let me know if anything slips or goes wrong. Or Russ needs attention. Okay?"

He had his orders. And like a good soldier, he nodded and got on the horse. His muscles protested…a lot. But he said nothing. Now that he knew Tori, he wasn't surprised that she took care of him as well as Russ. She would deny no one her care whether she was happy with him or not.

After making sure the door was firmly closed, Victoria mounted Snowflake and took Snoopy's reins to lead them down the trail. Jon imagined her shouting "Wagons, ho!" as they always did on television. He'd ride in her wagon train anytime. Not that he'd say that. He knew he wasn't supposed to say—or do—anything other than what she ordered. But maybe that stolen kiss would ease the pain he felt in his legs and butt from yesterday's long ride.

Something needed to.

AT TEN O'CLOCK, Tori found a level, grassy area to stop for a break. She wanted Russ to get his medicine when he needed it. So far, things had gone without a hitch, thank goodness.

She swung out of her saddle and walked to the litter. "How are you, Russ?"

He'd been asleep, and he looked at her blankly. "Tori?" he asked in a whisper.

"That's right. It's time for you to take your medicine and maybe take a break. Is the ride too bad?"

By that time, Jon had dismounted and he joined her at the litter in time to hear her question.

"If it is, I'll trade with you, buddy. My rear is going to be black and blue for a month, at least."

Russ almost managed a smile.

"I'm going to untie the litter, so keep him balanced until both sides are untied."

"Why are you untying it? I can get him out without doing that," Jon protested.

"But Jack can't eat with the litter in his face," she explained, continuing to untie the first side. Jon grabbed the pole as it came loose. Then, as she finished untying the second side, he lowered it to the ground, leaving Russ at a slant.

"Do we untie Snoopy, too?" he asked.

"Nope. Okay, Russ, we're going to get you up. Here are your boots." While he'd lowered the litter, she'd opened the bag and gotten Russ's boots

Jon unzipped the bag so he could find Russ's sock-covered feet.

"I don't have on jeans," Russ fretted.

"We thought you'd ride more comfortably without your jeans. I'm sure all the deer will blush, cousin, but I won't," Tori told him, hoping to see a smile. No such luck. She tossed him the blanket he'd been wrapped in that morning. She'd slipped it onto the litter under the tarp. "Preserve your modesty with that. But hurry up. We can't rest too long."

Jon helped him up once the boots were in place,

holding the blanket to shield him from Tori's eyes, then wrapping it around him. In the meantime, Tori untied Jack's reins and put them on the ground so the horse could graze.

"Do we have anything for lunch today?" Jon asked in a low voice.

"Yes." She didn't explain it was only peanut butter and jelly sandwiches. Any kind of meat would've spoiled by now.

She stretched out a little. Then she passed around the sandwiches. Russ showed no interest in his.

Jon gave Russ his pill. Then he asked, "How come the jelly hasn't bled through on the sandwiches? Mine always do."

"I coat both sides of the bread with peanut butter. Then I spread the jelly on and smash the sides of the bread together so the jelly can't get to the bread."

"Good thinking, Tori. I'll remember that."

She frowned at him and shook her head. Really! It wasn't rocket science. He was a doctor for heaven's sake. And a very patient one. He hadn't complained about anything the entire trip.

Once again they started down the trail. She had saved her sandwich for a late lunch. She planned to stop again at two. Unless everyone was doing well. Jon could give Russ his pill from the saddle and they'd only be a couple of hours away, maybe even less. She toyed with the idea of not stopping again. She'd have to wait and see.

There were a few level places where they could

pick up speed, but not many. The rain had stopped before their break, which helped matters.

When two o'clock rolled around, she stopped Snowflake and turned him halfway around. "Jon, how are you doing?"

"Fine."

She could tell he was lying, but she hoped he meant he could manage. "Is Russ awake?"

The trail was wide there, so Jon edged Devil forward a little. "No."

"Do you think you can make it without stopping?"

"Sure. How much farther?"

"We've gone a little faster than yesterday, so I think we can be down the mountain in about an hour. When we get to the top of the last ridge, I'll call the house. They can bring one of the SUVs and get you and Russ to the clinic quickly…with a much softer seat."

"What about the horses? They deserve—"

"They'll be taken care of. It'll be oats for all of them tonight." Snowflake nodded his head and whinnied, as if he understood.

Jon laughed. "Okay, I've been saving my cupcakes, but I think I'll have them now. Want me to give Russ his pill now, or let him sleep?"

"You're the doctor," she replied.

"Let's let him sleep. I'll start the antibiotics intravenously when we get him to the clinic."

Tori sighed. She paused, then looked him straight in the eye. "I want to thank you for your help. You haven't complained once and I know you're hurting.

I'm sure it's made a difference to Russ. And I want to forget everything else about this trip.'' She hoped she'd made herself clear.

He didn't say anything. And why should he? It was a guy's best dream, wasn't it? Free sex and no responsibility? Okay, so he didn't act that way now, but she wasn't going to discuss it ever again.

She turned away and started down the path to home.

They stopped one more time at the top of the last ridge. She pulled out her cell phone and dialed the ranch. "Red? It's Tori.''

Before she could say anything else, Pete spoke. "Tori? Did you find Russ?''

"Yes, Uncle Pete. He's with us. But…he's not doing so well. Dr. Wilson wants him in the clinic at once. Can you pick Russ and the doctor up at the bottom of the mountain and take them into town? It's been a long two days.''

"How is he?''

She heard the pain and anxiety in her uncle's voice and she tried to reassure him. "He's going to be okay. He's—run-down. He may have a light case of pneumonia.''

"Pneumonia? And he's riding? He may fall off. You can't—''

"Uncle Pete, he's safe, I promise. Just come get him.''

"I'll be there. And—thank you, sweetheart.''

She disconnected. "I don't think Uncle Pete is going to be mad. I was worried he would be.''

"Why would he? You saved your cousin's life. He told me, when we stopped, he only found the cabin because of the light in the window. He'd been lost since the day before."

She sighed. "Good. Now let's go home."

They exchanged a smile, a gentle smile that held no anger or distance. Then she urged Snowflake down the side of the mountain.

They saw several SUVs leave the ranch area and start crossing pastures, but it took a while for them to get down. The family was waiting for them as they rode down the crackback trails. Tori thought about how wonderful it was to know that all she had to do was call and her family would help her.

When she pulled Snowflake to a halt, she stayed in the saddle while Rich and his dad rushed to the litter. Jake and Brett began untying the litter. She saw Jon slide out of his saddle and then hang on to it, trying not to fall in front of everyone.

"Someone help Jon. He hasn't ridden that much and he's been terrific."

He glared at her, but she knew he needed the help. Samantha, Rich's wife, and Jake ran to his side. Janie was holding Russ's hand.

Samantha said, "I know how that feels. I thought I knew how to ride until I went out with these crazy people." She grinned. "I think they were all born on the back of a horse."

"Yeah," was all Jon could manage.

After they got the litter untied, and Jon and Russ

in one of the SUVs, Brett turned to her. "Aren't you getting down, baby girl?"

Her father hadn't called her that in a long time. She smiled at him. "I've got to take the horses in and reward them for a job well done," she said wearily.

Rich turned from the SUV where he was watching Russ. "I think I can do that job, Tori. You've already done the important one. We're grateful," he added in a gruff voice.

Tori knew he was trying to control his emotion.

"I'd enjoy the company," she returned with a smile.

Brett ordered, "Get in the other SUV, Tori. We're taking you back to the house to pamper you. Red and Mildred are cooking a feast for you."

She slowly slid out of the saddle. Her father was there to wrap his arms around her. Then Pete hugged her and thanked her again.

"I should've gone, but I promised him," he said shakily.

"I know, Uncle Pete, but I didn't," Tori whispered. "And we're all fine. That's what counts."

"Yeah," he muttered, then swung her into his arms and carried her to the front seat of the second vehicle.

Anna, after giving her daughter a hug, climbed into the vehicle with Jon and Russ, in case Jon needed help at the clinic. Jake and Rich mounted Snowflake and Devil and started the ride back to the barns. Uncle Chad and Aunt Megan, along with her dad and Samantha, were escorting Tori back home. Brett started the vehicle.

"You did good, Tori," Chad said quietly from the back seat. "We were all worried you wouldn't be able to remember where the cabin was."

"I was worried, too."

"Tori, honey, why didn't you get one of your cousins to go with you?" Megan asked, her voice gentle with no reproach.

"Because I knew Uncle Pete had made them all promise. I didn't want to force one of them to break his word to him. But I hadn't promised. I was going alone, but Jon figured out what I was doing and insisted on coming with me."

"Thank God," Chad muttered.

"I could've managed, Uncle Chad," she insisted, hurt by his words.

"I know you could have. But four hands are better than two. Making the litter and getting Russ on it would've been hard alone."

"Especially since you're such a little thing," her father added.

"Russ has lost a lot of weight," Tori muttered, frowning. "I don't think he took good care of himself the ten days he was gone. He—he hasn't really talked much. He told Jon that he'd lost his way the day before yesterday and had to spend the night in the forest. Then when we got there the next evening, I lit the kerosene lanterns and put one in the cabin window. That's how he got back to the cabin."

Megan gasped and reached over the seat to pat Tori's back. Chad shook his head. "Well, you were there for him, and Janie and Pete will never forget that.''

Tori rubbed her forehead, feeling a headache coming on. "I didn't want to lose him. We've already lost Abby. It would be too much."

"Yes," Megan agreed softly. "Too much."

JON GOT HIS PATIENT cleaned up and in bed. He then started an intravenous line with nutrients and antibiotics.

"Look, I'm going to run home and shower and put on clean clothes. Maybe shave myself," he added with a wry grin as he scraped his cheek. "Then I'll be back to check on him again."

"Can you come to the house this evening for dinner?" Janie asked.

"Frankly, Mrs. Randall—"

"Janie, please."

He nodded with a smile. "If I sit down, I'm going to fall asleep. I appreciate the offer, but I'll have to take a rain check. Besides, I want to keep an eye on Russ."

"But I'll stay and watch him," Anna said.

"Nope. The other nurse will stay until I get back. You need to take care of Tori. She was incredible. But it was a strain. She needs some nurturing. And I prescribe bed rest for her tomorrow. No working."

Anna beamed. "Yes, Doctor. We're going to keep her at the ranch tonight."

"Good. She's lost weight, too, since Abby's death.

I know it's been hard on all of you, but I want everyone eating three square meals a day, okay?''

"Yes, Doctor," Janie hurriedly agreed. "When will Russ get to come home?"

Jon shrugged his shoulders and then wished he hadn't. "I don't know. We'll see how he responds."

After kissing their son goodbye, Pete and Janie, accompanied by Anna, headed for the door. But Anna stopped beside Jon and gave him a hug. "Thank you for bringing Tori back safely."

"Believe me, Anna, it was the other way around." In fact, when he thought about what had happened, he felt horribly guilty. Tori seemed to hate him, but he hadn't forced her in any way. In fact, part of the pleasure had been her responsiveness. He needed to talk to her, to find out what was wrong.

And if she wouldn't talk to him, then he'd have to talk to Brett.

Chapter Nine

Jon stood propped against the wall across from the open door to Russ Randall's room, staring at his patient.

The nurses had reported that Russ was refusing to eat and had taken out the intravenous feed several times. So Jon was watching, trying to decide what to do. He'd only had him in the clinic for less than twenty-four hours, but he should be showing more improvement.

Twenty-four hours. Jon's body still ached from his trip up and down the mountain, in spite of long hot showers. He was glad he had gone, of course, for Russ's sake, though so far the man had shown no appreciation.

He was glad he had gone because of Tori, too. But he hadn't talked to Brett yet. First he wanted to talk to Tori. He'd missed her. She'd stayed at the ranch the night before and he'd felt lonely, knowing she wasn't next door.

That was silly. He couldn't get attached to her that

quickly. He paused. Their lovemaking had been so extraordinarily incredible, maybe he could.

Not that she'd let him touch her now.

He was startled to see her come around the corner and head in his direction.

"You're back," he called softly.

She stopped two feet from him. "How's Russ?"

"The same."

Her gaze sharpened. "He's been on antibiotics for twenty-four hours, hasn't he? Longer actually. You started the medication Saturday night and it's Monday afternoon. Why isn't he showing any improvement?"

Jon had told Russ's parents that morning to be patient, but he was rethinking his advice. "I can medicate Russ, honey, but I can't give him the will to live."

"Don't call me honey! What do you mean?"

"Russ is refusing to eat and he keeps removing the drip when no one's around."

She turned to study her cousin. "It's in now."

"Yeah. The nurse just put it back in ten minutes ago."

"When's his next meal?"

"In about fifteen minutes. It's almost six."

"What are you doing working so late?"

"I'm trying to figure out what to do with your cousin. After busting my butt to help you find him, I'm not too happy about his attitude." This morning his parents had patted him, consoled him, in fact, downright babied Russ. It hadn't done any good.

Tori drew a deep breath. "Excuse me."

Jon didn't move. He wanted to see the effect of Tori's visit on her cousin.

She strode up to the bed. "Russ Randall, what do you think you're doing?"

His hand had been creeping to the drip again. He jerked at the first sound of her voice. "Tori?"

"Yes, it's Tori. Why aren't you getting better?"

He shrugged his shoulders and said nothing.

Tori crossed her arms under her breasts, which disturbed Jon's focus. He remembered the silky softness, the—Tori reminded him of what was going on.

"I hear you're being a rotten patient."

Russ closed his eyes.

"Don't pretend you're sleeping, Russ. I never thought you were a coward." Her cheeks were red with temper.

"Hey!" Russ complained faintly.

"Hey, what? I thought you were a Randall. Randalls fight for what they get. How do you think the Randalls own so much land? Our great-grandfather fought for his land. Every generation has continued to fight. But you're giving up?"

"You don't understand! I don't want to live without Abby!"

"And you don't care about any of us? About your parents, your brothers Rich and Casey? What about me?" She leaned forward, resting her hands on either side of his pillow. "I went against Uncle Pete to find you. I need you, Russ. I'm in trouble and I need you! Are you just going to abandon me because it's too hard to live?"

"What's—wrong?"

Jon took a step toward the room. That was the first time he'd heard even an ounce of interest in Russ's voice.

Tori stood up and turned her back on Russ. "I can't tell you now. You obviously don't care."

"Tori—tell Rich. He'll help you."

"No. I can't. I can't believe you're quitting on me. Is this what Abby would want? If it had been you who had died, would you want her to quit? Would you want her to dump the gift of life and quit trying?"

"She—she was everything to me. It hurts—too much."

Tori turned around, tears streaming down her face. "Do you think I don't know that? I loved her, too. So did your parents. Will we hurt less when we have to bury you, too, because you were too selfish to try to live?"

"Tori—tell me your problem," he ordered, but his voice was weak.

"No. I guess it doesn't matter. It's certainly less important than your life." She turned and ran out of the room.

Jon moved quickly to the other side of the door. When she came around the corner, he slipped his hands beneath her arms and lifted her in the air.

"Way to go, tiger," he enthused softly.

"P-put me down," she whispered fiercely.

He slowly lowered her, beaming at her. "I think you may have awakened Russ to reality. Just what he needed."

She looked at him, then burst into tears and fell onto his chest. He wrapped his arms around her and held her tightly against him. ''Shh, baby, it's going to be all right. You fought again and I think you won.''

''What's wrong?'' Janie demanded behind Jon. She came around him and put an arm around Tori, too. ''Is it Russ?''

Tori turned into her aunt's arms. Pete joined them. ''What's wrong with Tori? How's Russ?''

Jon motioned them back down the hall, away from Russ's room. ''We've had a rough day. Russ has been trying to avoid getting well.''

''Why?''

Jon shrugged his shoulders. ''He said it was too painful to live.''

Janie moaned and covered her mouth, her eyes filling with tears.

''What are we going to do?'' Pete asked.

Jon grinned. ''I think Tori has already done it. She told him he was a coward and selfish. She pointed out that Abby wouldn't have wanted him to behave this way.''

Pete and Janie stared at Tori, stunned by what Jon had said.

She stiffened her shoulders. ''I know that was cruel, but I thought if I shocked him, maybe he'd think about what he was doing.''

''And?'' Pete asked.

Before Jon could say anything, a nurse hurried past them.

"Sandy? Where are you going?" Jon asked.

"Mr. Randall rang his bell, Doctor."

Jon nodded for her to continue on. "Let's see what Russ wants. I think that will tell us what we can do."

The nurse came back out again. When Jon raised an eyebrow, she whispered, "He wanted to know when he could get dinner. He's hungry."

"Oh, glory be," Janie said softly, tears falling down her cheeks.

Pete hugged her to him, and, over her head, he said, "Tori, thank you again."

"Don't thank me, Uncle Pete. I just reminded him of what y'all have taught us—to fight. I was slow to learn that lesson, but it's an important one."

"Well, you've sure got it down pat now," Jon said, grinning.

She backed away from all three of them. "I'd better go. I don't think he's going to want to see me for a while."

Though Janie and Pete protested, she was determined.

Jon called to her. "Will you be home this evening?"

"Yes, but I'm going to sleep early," she warned him.

That wasn't going to stop him, but he didn't let her know that.

"Can we go in and see Russ now?" Janie asked, her focus on her son.

"Sure." Jon let them go first, but he followed them in. He wanted to be sure Russ had decided to live.

They stayed for almost an hour. Janie hand-fed Russ his dinner. Jon left them alone for a while but continued to check on them.

After they had gone, he stepped into Russ's room. "Glad to see you're eating, Russ. At this rate, you'll recover faster than my muscles will from that ride."

"Mom and Dad said you came with Tori. I—I don't remember much." He closed his eyes.

"And I'll never forget it. Can I do anything for you before I go home for the night?" he asked as he took Russ's wrist and checked his pulse.

"No. I think I'll go to sleep soon."

"Good. The nurse will be here and she can call me if you need me."

"Thanks."

He left the room and walked to the nurse's desk. "I want you to check on Russ at least every two hours. If we're lucky, he'll sleep through the night, but he's been difficult today. So make sure he's on track. Call me for any reason. Okay?"

"Yes, Doctor."

He stopped by the café and got some food to go. He would get some for Tori, but he knew he had no chance of convincing her to join him.

After he ate, he strolled out his door and knocked on Tori's.

"Who is it?" she called, but he knew she knew it was him.

"Jon."

"Sorry, I'm already dressed for bed."

Several answers occurred to him. Like he'd seen

her naked, so what difference did it make. Or—never mind. He wasn't going to say that. "I want to tell you about Russ."

After a long pause, she said, "So, tell me."

"Through the door? I don't think so. If you don't care about—"

The door swung open and a highly irritated Tori glared at him.

"Interesting nightgown," he muttered. She was still fully dressed in blue jeans and a short-sleeved sweater.

Her cheeks flushed, making her look adorable, but that wasn't the mood she was in. "All right. Tell me about Russ."

"We do have some other things to discuss, too. I'll come in." Without waiting for an invitation, he pushed past her into the living room.

"Jon Wilson! You get out of my home!"

He sat down on the sofa and patted the spot beside him in invitation.

She clenched her teeth and fisted her hands.

"You'd better close the door before the bugs come in."

She practically slammed it off the hinges.

"Careful, you'll wake the neighborhood."

"There is no neighborhood except you, and I don't care if I disturb your sleep."

"Good thing," he muttered. Then he spoke louder. "Russ is doing fine. Pete and Janie stayed about an hour with him. He ate almost all his meal, and he agreed to have visitors."

Tori sank into a nearby chair as if her legs had given out. "Really? He's better?"

"Yeah, thanks to you."

She closed her eyes, her arms wrapped around herself, and tears escaped to roll down her cheeks. "Thank you."

"How are you feeling?" he asked softly.

Her eyes popped open and she wiped her cheeks dry. "Fine."

"Recovered from the ride?"

"Yes. How about you?"

He grinned. "I still ache whenever I move."

She said nothing in return.

He asked, "When is your next period due?"

She glared at him and rose to her feet. Walking over to the door, she opened it and stood there. "Please leave."

"Tori, all I'm suggesting is providing you with a pregnancy test. We have some at the office."

"No, thank you."

"Why?"

"I don't need one. Please leave."

"You can't be sure, certainly not this early."

She stopped being nice. "Get out! If you don't, I'll call the sheriff and have you thrown out."

"Okay, I'm going. But if you start feeling—"

She slammed the door after him before he could finish.

Okay. He'd go talk to Brett. She wouldn't talk to him, but he felt sure her father would. Brett would want him to be responsible.

TORI THREW HERSELF across her bed and cried. That miserable man! Why couldn't he leave her alone? She was glad to hear Russ had pulled himself together, but she didn't want to talk to Jon about their "incident" on the mountain.

That's all it was to him. She knew that. And she tried to tell herself that was all it was to her. But she hadn't convinced herself yet. When she slept last night, she'd dreamed of Jon and what they'd shared. She was afraid to go to sleep tonight. Especially after he came over.

And he was staying for four years.

How could she stand it? What was it about him that attracted her? He was handsome, of course, but there were other handsome men. He was strong, his muscled arms and chest showed that. He was patient, intelligent, gentle—ooh! She hated him!

AFTER A RESTLESS NIGHT, she got up the next morning at her regular time, to get ready to work. The phone rang, and she stared at it. Early-morning calls made her nervous.

"Hello?" she said cautiously.

"Darling, it's your mother."

"Hi, Mom. Is everything all right?"

"Of course, dear. But we need you to come to dinner tonight. We're having Jon for dinner to thank both of you, and, of course, you need to be here, too."

"Oh, no, I—"

"Of course you'll come. Besides, we need to decide what to do about July Fourth. It's only a week away, so if we're going to entertain as we usually do, we'll need to get organized.''

''Mom, I have a lot of work to do. Maybe another night.''

''No, it has to be tonight. Jon said you'd ride together. No sense in both of you driving out.''

''But, Mom—''

''Please don't argue, dear. I have a lot to do today.''

''Yes, Mom.'' Tori gave up. When the family called, she couldn't say no. But maybe she could convince Jon that he wanted to drive himself. Yes, that's what she'd do. She'd tell him she didn't need the ride when she went to the clinic. She was going to drop by to see Russ anyway. Hopefully, he was still talking to her.

And she could talk to Jon in front of several others and be safe. She hoped.

Half an hour before she was supposed to open the office, she walked to the clinic.

''Good morning, Faye,'' she said, smiling at the receptionist. ''I didn't know what time the clinic opened and I wanted to see my cousin. Can I go through here?''

''Of course,'' Faye told her.

Tori started through the door, and Faye said, ''Aren't you going to ask about the doctor?''

''Ask what about the doctor?'' she asked sharply.

''To see him. I'm sure he'll want to see you.''

''No. I'm not.''

"Shy, are you? I heard about him hugging you." Faye broke out a large grin. "Lucky you!"

"That was an accident!" Tori protested. "It meant nothing. We don't—I think he's seeing someone else."

"Really?" Faye said, leaning toward her, eagerness in her look. "I hadn't heard. Who is it?"

"I—I promised not to tell."

"Oh, come on, Tori. Tell me!"

"I have to hurry. I'll be late to work," she said, and rushed through the door and down the hallway. Damn Jon and his ridiculous behavior. Now the entire town would be talking. And she'd just told a lie. What was she going to do now?

Suddenly an idea struck her. Of course, she had intended to introduce him to the Waggoner sisters. She'd invite them to accompany her and Jon tonight. Perfect!

She managed to get to Russ's room without seeing anyone. Knocking hesitantly on the door, she said, "May I come in?"

Russ nodded.

"Are you still speaking to me?"

"Not only that, I'm going to thank you," he said, smiling.

"Oh, Russ, I'm so sorry I had to say those things," she said, rushing to the side of the bed and hugging his neck.

"According to Jon, you saved my life…twice."

"Don't pay any attention to him. When will you get out of the hospital?"

"It will be a few days yet. Jon says my chest hasn't cleared up yet. And I'm still weak. I don't remember much about our trip down the mountain. He said you made a litter so I didn't have to stay on Jack. I don't think I could've done that."

"No, probably not. I'm just glad you're back."

"Yeah," he agreed, but she couldn't see any enthusiasm in his face.

"Are you going to be all right?" she asked.

"Yeah. I don't have a choice. Someone I know told me I had to get well. By the way, what's the problem you need help with?"

She moved away from the bed. "Uh, I'll tell you…later. Not now."

"Why not now?"

"I can't."

Jon walked into the room, a cheerful smile on his face. "I heard you had the prettiest visitor in the place, Russ, so I thought I'd join you."

Tori turned her back to the two men.

"Tori, aren't you going to say hello?" Russ asked, a puzzled look on his face.

"Of course, good morning, Doctor."

She took several steps to the window and turned to lean against the windowsill, as far away from Jon as possible.

"I'm looking forward to this evening," Jon said, still smiling, but she noticed his eyes had narrowed.

"Oh, good." Then she smiled sweetly. "So am I."

His suspicious look pleased her. Now all she had to do was get to a phone and call her friends. They'd be grateful. After all, she was giving them first crack at the new doctor.

"Well," she said as casually as she could manage, "since you're doing so well, cousin, I'd better go open the office. We're a little behind, lazybones, so get out of the hospital as soon as you can. We miss you."

"We?"

"Oh, I forgot to tell you. I hired Jessica to be our receptionist until she goes back to school. I'm hoping by then we'll find a permanent one."

"Good idea."

Jon stopped her as she walked past him. "It will be a week before he gets out of here, I'm afraid. Even then, he'll have to start working only half days."

"We'll manage," she said, smiling at her cousin. "I'll check with you later."

"Good. We can talk," Russ said.

She didn't like the sound of that. "Sure. Bye."

Hurrying out, thinking she had gotten away, Tori almost jumped out of her skin when Jon caught her arm.

"In a hurry?"

"Yes, I am. I don't want to be late for work."

"Jessica will cover for you. How about a cup of coffee? I have some in my office."

"No, thank you."

"I told your mom we'd be there for dinner tonight at seven o'clock. So what time shall we go?"

"Six forty-five. Want to take my car?"

He had responded exactly as she'd expected him to. "No, I'll drive. I'll knock on your door."

Thank goodness she'd made a plan. "That's fine. Now I'll go."

"No goodbye kiss?" he teased.

"No. They're already gossiping about us, thanks to you."

"It doesn't matter."

"No, it doesn't, because I'm going to fix it."

Chapter Ten

"Jen? This is Tori Randall."

Jennifer Waggoner had gone to school with Tori. She and her sister had run the feed and general store in town since their dad's death about three years ago.

"Hi, Tori. Is there a problem with the books? You'll have to talk to Sarah about that, you know."

"No. I'm calling to ask you and Sarah to dinner out at the ranch tonight. The new doctor is coming, and I thought it would be a good idea for you and Sarah to meet him."

"I've heard he's a hunk."

"Mmm, yes, I suppose you could say that. Anyway, he hasn't met anyone but sick people. I figured he'll be thrilled to meet two beautiful single women."

"Well, with that kindly worded invitation, you can count me in. And Sarah, too. She has no social life, so I'm sure she's free."

"Great. Can you be at my apartment by a little after six-thirty?"

"Sure. We'll see you then."

She'd felt sure she could count on Jennifer to accept a social invitation. She liked her, but Jen and Jessica had more in common than Tori did. She was more partial to Sarah, the serious one. Sarah was a brunette. She was older and more responsible. In fact, Tori thought she worried too much, but she felt responsible for her sister, even though she was only three years older.

Tori quickly dialed the ranch house. "Mildred? It's Tori. I invited two more guests for this evening. Is that okay?"

"Of course." She paused and, with her hand over the receiver, she called, "Two more, Red." Then she turned back to Tori. "We're setting up extra tables now. Who's coming?"

"The Waggoner sisters. I thought it would be a treat for the doctor to meet them."

After a pause, Mildred said, "How generous of you."

"Er, yes. Um, do you want me to bring anything?"

"Nope. We got it covered. Oh, your mom's just pulling in. Want to talk to her?"

Definitely not. "No need. That's all I wanted. See you tonight." She quickly got off the phone.

"What are you up to?" Jessica asked, having heard both calls.

"Nothing you need to worry about, but if Mom calls, I'm in with a client and can't be disturbed."

As she hurried to her office, Jessica said, "You want me to lie to Mom?"

Tori looked over her shoulder. "It won't be the first time, little sister. I shared an apartment with you at college, remember?'' Tori laughed as her sister pouted.

The phone rang, and Tori hurried into her office and shut the door.

JON SHOWERED after he got home from the office. He shaved, too. This was his first invitation to the Randall ranch, and he wanted to make a good impression. Besides, he was going with Tori.

He was looking forward to the evening. They'd at least be alone during the ride. Maybe he could get her to talk a little. He could tell her Russ was making definite strides. That should please her.

But her acceptance of the evening told him she had something up her sleeve. He was beginning to read her like a book.

The phone rang and he tensed. What if she was calling to cancel their evening? The disappointment that filled him was a surprise. It was no big deal, right? But he knew better.

''Hello?''

''Son? How are you?''

''Dad! I'm fine. Kind of busy. Sorry I didn't call this weekend, but I went up into the mountains with a friend.''

''That's great. I've always wanted to see the Rockies.''

''Come on out. I've got a spare bedroom.''

''Aw, I couldn't leave Aunt Tabby on her own, you know.''

Jon heard the longing in his father's voice. His fa-

ther had loved his mother, but she'd demanded everything be centered around her. Jon didn't think he'd
ever heard his mother ask his father's preferences
about anything. After Jon's mother died, his uncle had
told his father it was his turn to care for Aunt Tabby,
Tabitha to everyone else.

His father had immediately moved the elderly lady
into his house and taken care of her.

"Aunt Tabby can travel, can't she? We'll share my
bedroom and Aunt Tabby can have the spare room.
Just let me know in advance so I can get a bed in
there."

"You think that would be all right? We wouldn't
be in your way? We wouldn't stay long, but I really
want to see those mountains. And you, of course."

"I'd love it, Dad. I think I can even arrange for
you to visit a real ranch, with cowboys and everything," he teased. "Think we can trust Aunt Tabby
around those sexy cowboys?"

"You find them sexy? You must've changed,
son," his father teased back.

Jon chuckled. "Nothing to worry about, Dad. The
cowgirls are even better."

"Oh, good. Let me talk to your great-aunt and see
if she'll come. I'd love to visit. When should we
come?"

"Whenever you can make it."

"Well, I never thought I'd get to see the mountains.
Just wait until I tell Tabby."

Jon checked his watch. "I have to go, Dad. I have

an invitation to dinner, but I'll call this weekend and see if you've made up your mind.''

He hung up the phone, grinning. His reason for insisting on going back to Chicago was to be with his dad, to ease the burden of Aunt Tabby a little. His father was only fifty-three. He might even remarry if he were free to meet someone. He owed him at least that opportunity.

Jon was finding himself happy in Rawhide, more than he'd ever thought he would be. The idea of settling down here wasn't a negative thing now, as it had been when he had arrived. And, really, Tori had nothing to do with that decision.

Right.

He pulled on a tweed coat over his white dress shirt and blue jeans and hurried out to Tori's door. He was right on time.

After knocking, he eagerly waited for her to answer. He hadn't seen her since morning and—

''Good evening, Jon,'' Tori greeted him, a smile on her face.

Jon thought he'd died and gone to heaven. Tori smiling at him was a sight to behold.

Then she stepped aside and waved to someone. Two women appeared behind her. ''I'd like you to meet Jennifer and Sarah Waggoner. They run the store in the next block.''

Even as he greeted them, he was wondering what their presence meant. Was Tori going to back out of the evening?

''They're going with us to dinner. I wanted you to

meet more citizens of Rawhide, so you'll feel more at home.'' Tori smiled again.

''I guess I'm the luckiest guy in Rawhide tonight, getting the chance to escort three beautiful women. Good evening, ladies. Are we ready?''

He wasn't surprised when Tori refused to ride in front with him, insisting Jennifer take that place, as one of their guests. Tori and Sarah, a pleasant-looking brunette, sat in the back.

He'd met women like Jennifer before. Easily entertained with flattery, interested in having a good time. Maybe he was misjudging her, but she seemed very young, more like Jessica. She needed seasoning to make her interesting.

He tried to listen to Tori and Sarah's quiet conversation in the back seat, but Jennifer kept up a running commentary on people in Rawhide, and he had to give up trying to hear them. It was a relief to reach the ranch.

There, he discovered even more Randalls than he'd already met. And he was introduced to Lavinia Dawson, Janie's mother, Russ's grandmother. It occurred to him that she might be a good person, along with Mildred, for Aunt Tabby to visit if she came. They seemed about the same age.

He received compliments and gratitude until he was thoroughly embarrassed. ''I promise you, I wouldn't have been able to make the trip without Tori. She was the master planner. I added a little muscle, but that was about it.''

To his surprise, Doc Jacoby appeared, too. ''You

know, boy, you made a hell of a house call. You're perfect for Rawhide.'' He lifted his coffee cup. ''Here's to a long stay.''

''Now, Doc, you know—''

''Yeah, yeah, I know. But plans change. Don't forget that.''

It occurred to Jon that he'd been thinking the same thing earlier this evening. But a visit was a lot different from his family moving here. He'd have to wait and see.

When they were to take their places for dinner, he was led to the seat on Jake's right-hand side, obviously a seat of prominence. He noted Tori took a place at a small table that seated six. He realized there were thirty people in the room.

''This is a lot of people to cook for,'' he murmured to Jake. ''I hope you didn't go to all this trouble just for me.''

''You saved one of us. Don't you think that deserves a celebration?'' Jake asked him.

''I couldn't save Abby,'' he reminded him quietly.

''You didn't have a chance. None of us did.''

''And Tori is the one who—''

''I know. She's a feisty little thing, isn't she?'' Jake said with a broad smile. ''She used to be quiet, almost afraid of her own shadow. I'd like to have heard her telling Russ off at the hospital.''

Jon grinned back. ''She was magnificent,'' he said.

''Make a good wife.''

Jon stared at Jake, surprised. Tori had said something about her family matchmaking, but he'd thought she was exaggerating. Jake was being even more direct than Doc and Anna had been.

Jake picked up a platter of steak and passed it to Jon. "Steak? Raised right here on the ranch."

The change of subject suited Jon just fine.

AFTER DINNER, everyone mingled. Jon noticed Tori was always on the other side of the room, no matter where he moved. Which made him decide tonight was when he should talk to Brett.

After looking around the room, he discovered Tori's father near the fireplace, talking to Griffin Randall.

As he walked up, Brett said, "Griff, have you met Dr. Jon Wilson?"

"Yes, I have. How are you?"

They stood talking for a few minutes. Then Griff was summoned across the room by his wife. Before anyone else could join them, Jon said, "I need to talk to you in private."

Brett studied him. "Okay. Let's take a stroll down to the barn. It gets warm in here with all these people."

The silence was a welcome relief. Until Jon thought about what he had to tell the man beside him. Brett stopped by a corral where several horses were prancing around. "What do you think of these guys? Toby is training them."

"To do what?"

"To be cutters." After looking at Jon, he realized the doctor had no idea what he meant. "Horses that can cut cows out of the herd and separate them. That's a useful talent for a cowboy's horse.''

''Oh. That's good. They're beautiful animals.''

''Yes. So, what do you need to tell me? Or is it to ask me?''

''I need to tell you something. You're not going to like it.''

Brett paused. Then he said, ''Okay.''

Jon hoped the man would be as calm when he finished. ''When Tori and I went up to find Russ...''

''Yeah?''

''When we got to the cabin, Russ wasn't there. Tori tried to hide how upset she was. We unpacked, settled in, ate dinner. Then when we were cleaning up, I tried to reassure her everything would be fine.'' He cleared his throat. ''Uh, things sort of escalated—we made love,'' he finished in a rush.

Brett took a deep breath. Then he snapped his mouth tightly together.

Jon figured he was about to receive a broken nose, but he couldn't deny the man his right.

When Brett said nothing, Jon said, ''I promise I didn't force her. In fact, it was mutual.''

''What are your plans?''

''Plans?'' Jon asked, not switching gears fast enough.

''Look, I know about emotions leading to—to sex. It happened to me and Anna. But I knew I wanted to marry her. I wasn't just, you know, scoring.''

''I'd marry her tomorrow if I could get her to at

least speak to me. But she won't. And she needs to. You see, we didn't use any protection.''

"You mean my daughter may be carrying an illegitimate baby?'' Brett demanded, his voice rising.

Jon clinched his jaw. "If there is a baby, it won't be illegitimate. I'll marry Tori long before the baby appears. I won't wait until she's ready to deliver. But if she won't even talk to me, I can't get to the root of the problem.''

"What? Why won't she talk to you?'' Brett asked.

Jon shrugged his shoulders. "I don't know. I can't even get her to listen to me, much less answer. All she'll say is she's not pregnant, and besides, it isn't necessary. I need someone to—persuade her to be reasonable.''

"Women!'' Brett said, frustration in his voice.

"Yeah,'' Jon agreed. "Oh, I have to tell you something else. I can't promise to keep her here in Rawhide if we marry. I have to go back to Chicago. I've got commitments there.''

"Another woman?'' Brett demanded, frowning.

"No, my family.''

"Boy, this is a mess.''

"Yes.''

"I'll have to talk to her mother and see what we should do. I'll let you know tomorrow.''

"I appreciate your help, Mr. Randall, and I'm sorry I let you down.''

Brett grunted. "It happens. But don't you hurt her!''

"No, sir.''

WHEN THE ALARM SOUNDED the next morning, Tori shut it off and then lay there, thinking about the previous night. She'd solved one problem. She hadn't been alone with Jon. She'd worried about it when they dropped the Waggoners off at their store. They lived above the store, as Tori and Jon lived above the accounting office.

Surprisingly, to Tori, Jon wasn't interested in conversation. He said he enjoyed her family, and the food was certainly good.

Then he told her good-night, waited until she'd unlocked her door and then entered his apartment. He didn't seem to care anymore if she was pregnant. Good thing she hadn't believed him!

At least they'd made a decision about July Fourth. They were going to have the celebration and ask Jon to keep Russ in the hospital until July fifth. Tori thought that would be best for Russ. He was doing better, but he couldn't handle facing all the condolences and sympathy just yet.

Finally she dressed and got ready to go downstairs. She had work to do. Just as she headed to the door, her phone rang. What was going on? She didn't usually get early-morning phone calls. First yesterday and then today.

"Hello?"

"Baby girl, are you dressed?"

"Daddy! I mean, Dad. Yes, I am. I'm going downstairs."

"Not yet. Your mother and I need to talk to you."

"Why?"

"Never mind. We're here. We'll be right up."

She hadn't made a pot of coffee, because Jessica would make a pot in the office and she'd get her coffee there. Now she changed her mind and began a pot of coffee. Before she finished, her parents knocked on her door.

She let them in with hugs and a smile. "Good morning. This is a nice surprise. I just put on coffee."

"Good," Anna said, "because I brought pastries from Red and Mildred."

"Oh, yum. I'm glad I didn't eat breakfast."

Her parents froze and exchanged a look. Tori had no idea what was going on, but something was.

"Will the smell of coffee bother you?" Brett asked.

"No. I hadn't made a pot here, because Jessica makes it downstairs." She frowned at them. "Will it bother you?"

"No," Brett snapped, and pulled out a chair at her table and sat down.

"Dad, what's wrong?"

The light on the coffeepot came on and her mother waved her to a seat. "I'll pour. Here's a plate for the pastries."

Tori stared at her. Anna's voice was gentle, sympathetic.

"If someone doesn't explain soon, I'm going to scream."

Brett growled, "Jon told us."

No. Her father couldn't mean what—Jon was a smart man. He wouldn't— "Told you what?"

"About the baby!" Brett yelled, rising to his feet.

Tori stood, too. "What baby?" she shouted in response.

"The one you may have made up on the mountain!" Brett bellowed.

Anna intervened. She put a cup of coffee in front of her husband, then one in front of her daughter. "Take a deep breath and let's discuss this calmly." They both sat down.

"I can't believe he told you. Why would he do that?"

"Because he's a responsible man. My daughter *should* have told me!" Brett said, his temper rising again.

Tori rolled her eyes toward her mother. "Mom, please, he's not being realistic."

"I know, dear, but it's difficult for a father to realize his daughter is—is doing the same thing he's, uh, doing."

"It's different! We're married! That's more than you can say, baby girl!"

"True. And it's good to know my parents remained chaste and pure until their wedding day." She stared at her father. She didn't know for sure, but she'd heard enough teasing between the brothers and their wives to suspect things.

Her father's face turned bright red. "That's none of your business!"

"I agree. And my activities are none of your business."

"She's got you there, sweetheart," Anna said with a grin.

"We're not here to talk about what you did," Brett returned, surprising her.

"Then why are we talking about it?"

"It's the pregnancy test," Brett said. "Jon said you wouldn't take one."

Tori raised her chin. "That's because I'm not pregnant."

"How do you know?" Brett quickly returned.

"I just do," Tori said stubbornly.

"Darling, I'm on your side, you know," Anna said softly. "But I'm a nurse and I don't buy that response. It's too soon for you to be feeling any of the symptoms."

Tori got up from the table and turned her back to her parents. "It doesn't matter."

"What does that mean?" Brett demanded.

Tori turned and faced them. "It means that if I'm pregnant, I can take care of my baby. And if I'm not pregnant, then everything's fine."

"I'm not having any illegitimate babies in my family!" Brett roared.

"You want me to change my name?" Tori asked, hurt.

"Yeah, I do, by marrying the doctor. He said he'd marry you if you're pregnant."

She thought she'd die of embarrassment. Her father had insisted Jon marry her?

"I can't believe you did that," Tori said, beginning to pace.

"I didn't force him. He told me he intended to marry you if you were pregnant."

She was going to kill the doctor. "He's wrong. He's not going to marry me for any reason."

"What?" Brett roared.

Tori folded her arms. "Dad, I appreciate your concern. But I make the decisions about me and any possible baby. If I am pregnant, I'll either move away or—or change my name, if you don't want us around."

Brett stared at her. "Of course, I want you around. You know I don't really mean that, baby girl!" He moved quickly and wrapped his arms around her. "In fact, that's the one thing that bothered me. He's planning on taking you back to Chicago if he marries you."

"Well, I'm not going to Chicago, so you have nothing to worry about," Tori assured him, tears in her eyes.

Anna came around the table and joined in the group hug. "I didn't want you to leave, either. Chicago! That would be horrible."

"This is all Jon's fault. I want you to go back home and forget about all of this. If I have a problem, I'll let you know. If the doctor complains, just ignore him."

"But, darling, this would all be over if you took the test after two weeks," Anna reminded her.

"I know," she said softly. Then she wiped the tears away. "Now, I'm going to visit a certain doctor and explain the facts of life to him. Sorry I upset you both.''

She strode out of her apartment, a determined look on her face.

Chapter Eleven

The walk to the clinic wasn't long. But it was long enough to make Tori realize she didn't want to confront the doctor in front of an audience. She didn't want to confront him at all. She knew she'd have to take a test, ultimately, but it was too early. When it was necessary, she'd do it. But she wanted him to leave her alone until then.

He began seeing patients at nine o'clock. She had ten minutes to inform him, privately, that he'd have a war on his hands if he dared reveal their secrets publicly. And that she had no desire to marry him. A reluctant bridegroom would not be her idea of happiness.

If he loved her—she dropped that thought at once. It wasn't in the realm of possibilities. She never intended to marry unless she and her future husband loved each other, like her mother and father.

Totally. Completely. Forever.

Not for four years. Because she wasn't living in Chicago.

"Good morning, Faye," Tori said, forcing the

smile on her face. "I know it's before nine, but would it be possible for me to see the doctor?"

Faye lifted the phone as she said, "I'll check," a big smile on her face.

Almost before she had hung up the phone, the door opened and Jon appeared. "Tori? What's wrong?"

She fought to keep the calm smile on her lips. "May I see you in your office, Doctor?"

He glanced at Faye and stepped back, waving her through the door that led to his office. Once they'd reached his office and he'd closed the door behind both of them, he asked again, "What's wrong? Are you sick? Did you throw up this morning?"

"No! But I felt like it, because my parents came to see me to talk about my unborn child."

"You wouldn't talk to me. I thought you should talk to someone."

"Jon, I'm an adult. I get to make decisions for myself."

"*I* felt it only right to tell your dad. *You* weren't being reasonable."

"How dare you! You had no right to tell him! That was my business!"

"But you weren't going to tell him, were you? You were stonewalling me. I had to do something."

"Do you have *any* brains?" she demanded. "Now you've gotten yourself in worse trouble!"

"What do you mean, worse trouble?"

"If I'm pregnant, my father is expecting you to marry me!" she snapped, sure she would upset him now.

Instead, Jon remained calm. "Of course he does. I told him I'd be marrying you if you're pregnant."

"Maybe you should buy *him* an engagement ring, because he's the only one in favor of marriage." It was a great exit line and she whirled to leave his office. But he was fast and blocked the door.

"What are you saying now? That you don't intend to marry me if you're pregnant?"

"I guess you have brains after all. You got that right!"

"Oh, I did, did I? Well, think again, Tori. My child is not going to be born illegitimate."

"Why do you think I told you it didn't matter?" She lifted her chin. "I'll raise my child. I don't need a man to do that."

"We'll see what the court says!" he snapped.

It hadn't occurred to her that he would fight that hard for a child he didn't want. Holding back tears, she went around him and opened the door. "I'm going to visit Russ."

JON STOOD THERE, his hands on his hips. She didn't expect him to marry her? What was wrong with her? Did she have that low an opinion of him? That he would father a child and ignore it?

He wasn't that kind of man.

Spinning on his heel, he hurried to the clinic.

"Doctor?" one of his nurses called to him as he left his office. "Aren't you ready to see patients?"

"I'll be back in a minute. There's something I need to do."

When he got to Russ's room, Tori was sitting on the edge of her cousin's bed, chatting calmly.

Jon didn't hesitate. "Russ, I need your help."

Tori almost fell off the bed. She caught herself and glared at Jon. "Don't you dare say anything! Russ has too many problems right now to worry about—about anything else."

Russ had made some progress, but he was struggling, frequently fading into listlessness, overcome by depression. Now his gaze sharpened. "What problem? Is this what you were talking about the other day, Tori?"

"No! There was no problem. I just wanted to get your attention."

"She's lying, Russ. There's a problem."

Though he'd planted himself in front of the door, Jon could see Tori wanted to run. "Go ahead, Tori. I'll just tell him after you're gone."

"I'm sure you will. You're no gentleman, Jon Wilson. You're not supposed to kiss and tell!"

"He kissed you?" Russ asked.

"I did more than that, Russ. It wasn't planned, but I was comforting her because you weren't in the cabin and—and things got out of hand."

Tori turned her back to both men, staring out the window. "I can't believe you're telling the world!"

"I'm trying to get you to be reasonable."

"Okay," Russ protested, holding up a hand as if he were directing traffic. "I can't say I'm happy about this. Not that I have anything against you, Jon, but

Tori's like my sister, and I don't want anyone taking advantage of her. Now, what's the problem?''

''I intend to marry her if she's pregnant.'' He saw relief in Russ's eyes. He shifted his gaze to Tori, but there was no acceptance on her face.

''Good,'' Russ said calmly.

Tori's head snapped up. ''Good? Good! You think that's a good idea? Men!'' She ran from the room.

Russ's eyes widened and he stared after her. ''What did I say to upset her?''

''You were reasonable. But she says she's not marrying me for any reason. She thinks I'm going to walk away from my own child. I promise you I'm not.''

''And that upsets her?''

''Yeah. She won't even agree to take a pregnancy test.''

''Isn't it a bit too soon?'' Russ asked, wincing a little as he thought about Abby explaining when she'd take a test.

''Yeah. But she refuses to take it whenever. She says it doesn't matter.''

''What does that mean?''

''That she'll take care of her child and it's none of my business.'' Jon paced around the bed and back again. ''I don't know what to do.''

Russ lay there in his bed, a frown on his face. ''Give me a couple of hours. Come back at lunch. I'm going to talk to Rich and Toby. They may have some ideas.''

Jon shook Russ's hand. ''Thanks, Russ. I need all the help I can get. I'll be back at noon.''

"JESS?" Tori called from her office. She'd worked hard all morning, but nothing was going right. She suddenly felt tired. "Would you go to the café and pick up lunch? I'll pay."

Jessica appeared in the doorway. "Sure. What do you want?"

"I'll take the chef salad and a soda. And don't forget some crackers. Here's a twenty."

"Oh, good," Jessica said with a grin. "Today's pie is coconut cream. That's enough money to pay for two pieces of pie. Okay?"

Tori nodded. "That's fine." In actual fact, she didn't care. Maybe the sugar would give her some energy. She had to get more work done. She'd spent an inordinate amount of time on the doctors' books. She still had the Waggoners' books to do.

As Jessica started out the door, Tori stopped her. "Jess, thank you for being here."

"It's good spending the day together, sis. I'll be back in a few minutes."

Tori's phone rang and she waved Jessica to go while she answered. Jennifer Waggoner greeted her.

"I just wanted to thank you for the invite last night. Sarah and I both had fun."

"I'm glad you enjoyed it. And you'll be at the Fourth party, won't you?"

"We wouldn't miss it! Everyone will be there, as usual."

"Yeah," Tori said with no enthusiasm at all. She'd like to stay hidden in her apartment.

"Are you interested in the doctor? He's very handsome. And doctors make a good living, even here in Rawhide.'' When Tori said nothing, Jennifer continued. ''I liked him, but I don't want to poach.''

''Feel free, Jen. That's why I invited you and Sarah. You don't think I'd introduce either of you to someone I was interested in until I had a ring on my finger, do you?'' Tori asked with a forced chuckle.

''You sure?'' Jen asked, obviously picking up on the strained sound of her voice.

''Definitely.''

She'd answered the phone at Jessica's desk, and she turned around when she heard the office door open. Two of her cousins came in, smiling at her.

''Uh, Jen, thanks for calling, but I've got company. I'll see you on the Fourth, if not before.''

When she hung up the receiver, she greeted her cousins. ''What are you two doing here in the middle of the day? Is there a problem?''

Toby and Rich exchanged a look. Toby answered, ''Well, it appears there is.''

Tori tensed up at once. ''Samantha? Elizabeth? Who is it?''

Rich looked at her. ''It's you, Tori.''

''What are you talking about? There's nothing wrong with me!''

''Russ called us.'' Toby watched the horror appear on her face. ''Yeah, it's about the doctor. We're supposed to talk to you.''

She almost fell into Jessica's chair and covered her face with her hands. ''No, no, no!''

''Hi, guys,'' Jessica called as she pushed her way

into the office, her hands full. "Are you here for lunch? I'm not sharing my pie. You'll have to go get your own." She smiled, not really worried about their appearance.

"Not today," Rich said, though he did take a sniff of the air.

"We're here to talk to Tori," Toby said.

Jessica asked, "There's nothing wrong at home, is there?"

"No, everything's fine."

"Then why—Mom and Dad came this morning. What's going on? And why is it being kept from me? Tori? What have you done?"

Tori stared at Toby. "Do you see what you've done? Just go home. I don't need your advice."

Toby stared at her. "Jon wasn't as difficult. He was willing to listen to our advice."

"You gave Jon advice about me? What did you tell him, Toby? Tell me!"

"Now, Tori, that wouldn't be fair. I mean, he wouldn't—"

Tori couldn't believe her personal life was being discussed by the entire family without her consent.

Jessica leaned in closer. "What fun! And this time you have to tell me what you've done, Tori! I always got in trouble, but you were the perfect child. I'm glad you're in trouble and not me, finally." She beamed at her sister.

Then she opened up the salad Tori had asked for and shoved it toward her.

Tori got one whiff of the salad and her poor, rebellious stomach heaved.

"I'M TELLING YOU, Russ, she puked on Jess's desk. Couldn't even eat her lunch," Rich said. "Just like Sam did when she first told me about the baby. We didn't get a chance to talk to Tori. She went to her apartment and locked the door."

"So you think she's pregnant?"

"I guess so, though you know Tori was always the first to get sick. She was the first one to have the chicken pox when Uncle Griff and Aunt Camille kept us. She could have the flu."

"Damn. I'm going to call Jon. Maybe he doesn't have any patients this afternoon and he can go check on her."

"Good idea. Think he'll take our advice?" Rich asked.

"I don't know why not. He didn't have any idea what to do. At least your advice makes sense. Thanks for trying."

For the first time since he'd come down the mountain, Russ wished he could hop out of bed and take care of things. He didn't want Tori sick or hurt. He rang the bell for the nurse.

A voice answered his call. "Yes, Mr. Randall? How may I help you?"

"I need to see Dr. Wilson."

"What's the matter? Has your intravenous needle come out again? I'll be right there."

"No! I want Dr. Wilson."

But there was no answer. A couple of seconds later, a nurse was in his room.

She examined the needle in his hand. "It seems all right. Do you have pain?"

"No. I just need to talk to Dr. Wilson."

"He was here only a few minutes ago, Mr. Randall. He does have other patients, you know," she said with a patronizing smile that irritated him.

"If you don't ask Dr. Wilson to see me when he can, I'm going to walk to his office."

"Now, now, Mr. Randall, you know you're too weak for that."

"Maybe so, but if I fall, you'll have to tell the doctor you wouldn't listen to me. You think he's going to be a happy camper then?"

"I don't appreciate threats, Mr. Randall. You'll stay in your bed, do you hear me? I'll call his nurse and tell her to send him over when he has time. But I won't have you calling him every time you hiccup!"

"Call the nurse from here," he snapped, determined to hear the call. Otherwise he figured the nurse wouldn't make the call until five o'clock.

"Very well!" she snapped in return. She deliberately made the call a non-emergency, but Russ figured Jon would at least call him right away.

"Thank you," he said when she finished. She glared at him and stalked out of the room. He smiled. It felt sort of good to go a round or two and win, no matter who his opponent was.

Two minutes later, Jon entered his room. "What is it?"

"Rich called. They didn't get to talk with Tori because she threw up, didn't even eat her lunch. Then she went upstairs and locked her door. I wondered if you could check on her when you're finished for the day.

"I don't have any patients for the next hour. I'll go at once."

As Jon headed for the door, Russ called him back. "Here's a key that opens both doors. I'm afraid she won't let you in. But…take it easy on her, okay?"

"Yeah, thanks."

Russ lay back down on his pillow, satisfied that he'd done his best for Tori.

TORI POURED HERSELF a glass of milk when she got upstairs. It had always calmed her stomach when she got too tense. And today had been full of tension.

Then she lay down on the couch and turned on some soothing music. A knock at the door alarmed her. "Who is it?"

"Tori, it's me, Jess. I have your lunch here."

"Throw it out. And close the office and go home."

"Tori, I'm sorry. You know I don't really want you in trouble. I was just teasing. Please take your lunch."

She heard the strain in her sister's voice. Great! Now Jessica was upset, too. She got off the couch and opened the door, checking to be sure it was only Jessica.

"Honey, everything's all right, I promise. I just got a little too upset. And I'm sorry I left it to you to clean up." She did feel guilty about that. Poor Jess.

"Will you eat your lunch? Mom will be upset if you don't."

"Jessica," Tori said, sternly this time, "I'm an adult. You don't have to tell Mom if I don't eat my lunch."

"Okay. I won't tell."

With a deep sigh, Tori thanked her sister. "I meant it that you could go home early. I'm going to take a rest."

Jessica offered to keep the office open. "I have some work that I can be doing."

"The world won't end if you don't get it done today. I'm sure everyone will cut us some slack under the circumstances. And if you work, I'll feel guilty for not working."

"Okay, I'll go home." She paused after opening the door. "But you know Mom is going to ask about it. So don't be surprised if she calls."

"I know, but do the best you can. Tell her I decided to take a rest because of all the strain and if she calls, she'll wake me up."

"Ooh, good thinking," Jessica exclaimed.

She turned to go, opening the door. Tori closed her eyes, glad to be alone at last.

"Hi, Jessica," said a deep, immediately recognizable voice. "Is your sister home?"

"Sure. Come in. Tori, it's Jon."

Tori didn't waste any time. "Go away."

"Tori!" Jessica protested, shock in her voice. "That was rude."

"Good. That's what I intended. Show him out, Jess."

She covered her face again, hoping her sister would do as she asked. When she heard the door close, she looked up to thank Jessica, only to find Jon standing in her place. "What did you do with Jessica?"

"She's gone home. How are you?"

"I'm fine. Why aren't you with your patients?"

"I heard I had a patient here."

"Damn! My family again! What did they tell you?"

"That you threw up your lunch."

"And, of course, you immediately decided I was pregnant? I'm not. I have a sensitive stomach. When I get upset, I can't keep anything down!"

"You're sure?" he asked, coming closer.

"I'm sure."

But he didn't leave. Instead, he sat down on the edge of the sofa and took her wrist in his hand. "Your pulse is a little elevated."

"Big surprise. Why would I be calm around you? You've caused me to be tense all day!"

"I'm sorry, sweetheart. I didn't mean to upset you."

"What a crock! No, all you wanted was for me to do whatever you wanted. Or else you'll keep my entire family stirred up!"

"Have you finished your lunch?"

"No! I'm drinking a glass of milk to calm my nerves, and I'm taking a nap—as soon as you leave."

He got up and she hoped he was leaving. Instead,

he stood behind her and put his hands on her shoulders. "I'm going to give you a neck rub to get rid of the tension, okay? Just relax."

"I don't want you to give me a..." Her protest finished with a sigh as his fingers began to rub her neck. It reminded her too much of his touch when they had been alone in the cabin. It made her vulnerable.

He began to work magic with his fingers. In spite of herself, she realized he was having a positive effect on her. After a few minutes, he pulled her from her chair.

"What are you doing?" she demanded, tense again.

"I'm taking you to your bed," he said softly.

Tori tried to retrieve her anger quickly enough to protest, but she couldn't. His massage had felt too good. "I—I don't think..."

"Tori, I meant I was taking you to your bed so you could go to sleep. All this tension isn't good for you. You need to relax."

"I'll relax when you get out of here."

"Do you promise?"

"Oh, yes. So, just be on your way."

He smiled. "Okay. There's just one thing I need to do before I go."

"What's that?" she said with a frown.

"Kiss you goodbye." Without another word, he took her lips in a strong, deep kiss, one that reawakened the desire they'd shared in the cabin. A kiss that wiped away his obnoxious behavior when he'd realized they hadn't used protection. A kiss that matched the dreams she'd been experiencing since that night.

He lifted his head, breathing heavily. "I'll see you tonight," he whispered. Then he left her alone.

So, the end result was the same.

She was alone with her dreams.

Chapter Twelve

Jon checked to make sure he hadn't forgotten anything. Popcorn, juice, two packages of cupcakes. He'd showered and shaved since he'd gotten home.

Checking his watch, he knew it was time. With everything in a sack, he swung open his apartment door...only to discover Jennifer Waggoner standing there, her hand raised, as if she'd been about to knock.

"Jon!"

"Uh, hi, Jennifer. Do you have an emergency?" He couldn't think of any other reason she'd be at his door.

"No, not an emergency, unless you consider boredom in that category. I went for a walk and decided to stop by."

He quickly surveyed her. Her hair was curled, her face made up and she was wearing a dress that he figured was date bait. Uh-oh.

"Um, well, you can join me and Tori. We're watching a movie tonight. One of my favorites is coming on." It suddenly occurred to him that Jennifer's presence might make Tori let him in.

"Oh, really? I don't want to intrude."

"Not at all. Knock on Tori's door for me, will you? My hands are full."

"Who is it?" Tori called through the wooden door.

"It's Jennifer and—"

The door opened. "Jennifer, what are you—Jon."

"Jon asked me to join you two to watch his favorite movie. I hope you don't mind. I didn't even think to ask the name of the movie, I'm so desperate for entertainment."

Jon licked his dry lips. "I didn't think you'd mind since I have only a small black-and-white television set. The movie is set in Paris and black-and-white just doesn't do justice to Paris."

Jennifer looked over her shoulder at him, frowning. Apparently she was realizing Tori didn't know he was coming. But to Jon's relief, Tori stepped back in invitation. "Of course I don't mind. Just what is this movie that's so great, Jon?"

"*Charade*. It's an old Cary Grant and Audrey Hepburn movie. Have you seen it?"

"Yes, it's wonderful."

Satisfaction swept through Jon. They had the same taste in movies. "I brought some snacks, too." He set the sack down on her breakfast table and pulled out the popcorn and the cupcakes. Then he set a bottle of fruit juice beside them. "I figured we'd need something healthy with the cupcakes." He leaned closer to Tori as Jennifer settled on the sofa. "I'll run back to my apartment and get more cupcakes," he whispered.

She shook her head and opened her pantry to take out another package. "No need."

"Didn't you bring any soda?" Jennifer asked. "It goes better with popcorn."

"What kind do you like?" Tori asked. "I have some."

Jon stood in the kitchen, watching while Tori fixed the soda for Jennifer. He wasn't going to sit down beside Jennifer. "May I put the popcorn in the microwave?"

"Of course."

Then he crossed to the television and turned it on, finding the right channel. The distinctive music came on. Returning to the kitchen, he asked for a bowl for the popcorn. Then he said, "Take Jennifer's soda to her. I'll bring in the popcorn when it's ready, along with the juice."

"And if I want a soda?" she asked, a challenge in her eyes.

"Then I'll fix you a soda. I thought juice might be easier on your sensitive stomach. How are you feeling, by the way?" He'd kept his voice low and Jennifer was staring at them.

"Need any help?" she called from the sofa.

"No, thanks," Tori said. Then she gathered up the packets of cupcakes and Jennifer's drink and headed to the sofa.

Jon poured the popcorn into a large bowl and fixed two glasses of juice. Then he found a place on the sofa beside Tori.

Jennifer stared at him. "Well, I'm going to have to

get closer to the popcorn. I just love it." She jumped up and came around the sofa to Jon's other side.

Tori stood up. "Here, Jen, take my place. I'm eating my cupcakes right now."

Jon ground his teeth. What was wrong with her? Tori knew he wanted to sit by her, didn't she? Maybe not. But if she was trying to matchmake, he was going to have a talk with her. Unable to do anything else, he scooted over, closer to Tori, leaving plenty of room for Jennifer.

When the movie ended at ten, two of the three people watching were completely frustrated. Jon hadn't had any privacy with Tori. And Jennifer had fared similarly with Jon.

She, however, hadn't given up. She thanked Tori for letting her join them. Then she turned to Jon. "Would you mind walking me home, Jon? The darkness scares me a little."

He didn't ask why she went out after dark if it scared her. His father had raised him to be a gentleman. "Of course I will."

Tori walked them to the door, and Jon bent down to kiss her cheek. "I won't be long."

Jennifer's gaze widened. "Oh, I'm sorry. Did you two have something planned?"

"Not at all," Tori said.

"She worries if I'm gone at night," Jon said, ignoring Tori's glare.

He took long strides on the one-block walk to the store. "It's convenient living over the store, isn't it?

In Chicago, we spent a lot of time on the Ell or taking taxis.''

Jennifer shrugged. Maybe she was too out of breath to answer. ''We're walking a little fast.''

''Sorry, I make hospital rounds at seven in the morning. A doctor's life is difficult.''

''But I always hear about doctors playing a lot of golf. Surely you have free time.''

''Not much. I don't know of any golf courses here.''

''There's one about an hour from here. I'd be glad to show you. In fact, I could take you around the county, give you a guided tour, if you'd like?''

''That's nice of you to offer, but I don't have time.''

''You had time to go up into the mountains with Tori,'' she retorted, irritation in her voice.

''I had to see my patient.''

They'd reached the store and he stood there, waiting for her to open the door.

She looked up at him. ''Well, thanks for escorting me. I hope I didn't keep you from your bed.''

He smiled.

Suddenly she leaned against him and got on her tiptoes to kiss him. He managed to turn his head, taking the kiss on his cheek. ''Night, Jennifer.''

Then he jogged away. ''Whew! That was a close call,'' he muttered to himself. He realized his reaction would have been quite different if it had been Tori wanting to kiss him. Just the thought of her touching him made him move faster.

As soon as he got back to their building, he jogged up the stairs to knock on Tori's door.

"Who is it?" she called.

"It's me," he replied. He was pleased when she opened the door. Of course, she didn't invite him in, but he didn't expect that she would.

"That was a fast trip."

"Yeah. Are you feeling all right?"

"Yes. I had a nap this afternoon, recommended by my doctor," she told him, grinning.

"Good."

"Jon, I'm sure Jennifer would have invited you to her place to see the movie. They just got a big-screen television, so you'll know in the future."

"I didn't invite her to come to your place tonight. At least, I did, but I didn't intend to. I'm glad you liked the movie, though."

"It's one of my favorites, too."

"Yeah, we have a lot in common."

"Right. One movie." She started closing the door. "Good night, Jon."

"Wait! Uh, we both like cupcakes."

She paused, leaving three inches of space between the door and the wall. "Yes, we do, along with a million other people. Otherwise that company would go broke."

"Yeah, but it counts."

She grinned. "Okay, cupcakes and movies."

"Yeah." He couldn't think of anything else to say, except "I'll see you tomorrow."

She raised her eyebrows. "Okay." Then she shut the door.

Jon stood there in the moonlight, wishing he'd thought of something more intelligent to keep her talking. But he hadn't. He unlocked his apartment door and got ready for bed.

Maybe it was best he'd had a chaperon tonight. Her cousins had told him to make friends with her. Then they could work something out. It was the first time he'd realized they hadn't spent enough time together for the intimacy they'd shared.

The night they'd made love, it had seemed so right, so perfect. Until he'd announced they hadn't used protection. He'd been mad at himself, but he hadn't explained that to Tori. Tonight had been good. He'd spent the evening with her. They'd liked the same movie.

He crawled into bed. When he closed his eyes, all he saw was Tori. All he thought about was Tori. All he wanted was Tori.

TORI AND JESSICA WERE closing the office for lunch the next day when a stranger appeared. It wasn't often that they saw strangers walking around.

Tori gave him a smile and a nod as Jessica was locking the door.

They'd had a good morning, calm and quiet, and she'd gotten a lot of work done without any problems. She was feeling good today.

"Uh, miss?" the man asked.

Since he looked nice, just a little older than her

dad, Tori assumed he was trying to find someone. "Yes?"

"I'm looking for the doctor."

"Is something wrong? Are you ill?" she asked.

With surprising vibrancy, he said, "I'm looking for my son."

"Does he live around here?" Jessica asked, just as confused as Tori.

"Of course he does. He's the new doctor."

"Jon?" Tori gasped. "You're looking for Jon?"

"Yes, I am. Do you know him?"

"Uh, yes," Tori responded cautiously. "He didn't tell us he was having a visitor. But the clinic is only a couple of blocks away." She pointed toward the building.

The man heaved a sigh. "Anywhere I can call him?"

Tori gave him an alternate choice. "Why don't you come to the café across the street and join us for lunch? We'll call Jon and have him come meet you."

"Will that be okay? I don't want to cause him any trouble. I left him a message last night. And this is his address." The man looked around, puzzled.

"You're right," Tori assured him. "His apartment is on the second floor."

"Thanks for the information, and I *am* hungry. You won't mind if I join you?"

With a shake of her head, Tori motioned toward the café. The man fell into step with them. "Are you Jon's father?" she asked, studying him.

"Yes, I am," he announced, pride in his gaze.

She escorted him and Jessica to a booth. "Look at the menu and I'll go call Jon."

"Tell him not to hurry on my part," the man insisted, frowning again.

Tori smiled and nodded. Then she crossed over to the counter. "Mona? Can I borrow your phone for a minute?"

"Sure, hon."

When Faye answered, she asked to speak with Jon.

"The doctor's with a patient, Tori. Can you wait a minute?"

"Yes, of course." She could leave a message, but she was afraid the visitor would be a shock.

Almost at once, he spoke. "Hello?"

"Jon, it's Tori."

"What's wrong? Are you feeling ill? I'll be right there."

"Jon, wait. You mustn't assume I'm sick every time you see me. I'm really very healthy."

"And you called to chat?" he asked, raising his voice in disbelief.

"Well, no, not exactly. Uh, were you expecting a visitor?"

"Visitor? Is your father there? Has he decided to punch my nose after all?"

"No. I'm talking about your father."

"What? Dad talked about maybe coming soon, but—is he accompanied by a fussy old lady?"

"No, it's just him, Jon."

"Where?" he asked, sounding bewildered.

"At the café with me and Jessica, having lunch. He decided to eat with us while I called you."

"I'll be right there."

Mona was at the table, taking orders, when Tori returned to the table.

"Did you talk to him?" Bill Wilson asked.

"Yes. He's on his way."

"You ready to order, Tori?" Mona asked.

"Yes, I'll have my usual salad, and bring the meat loaf for Jon."

"The doc? Yep, that's his favorite. Will he want creamed potatoes with gravy, or French fries?"

"Creamed," Tori guessed. "And two iced teas."

Mona walked away and Bill Wilson looked at Tori. "You already know his favorites?"

"Um, the waitress knew them, too," she pointed out.

Even Jessica was staring at her, surprise on her face, when Jon scooted into the booth beside her, his arm going around Tori's shoulders.

"Hello, Dad. Welcome to Rawhide."

Tori immediately shrugged against his arm, but he ignored her.

Jon looked at his father. "Why didn't you let me know you were coming?"

"I left you a message last night. Aunt Tabitha got invited to take a vacation with a friend. I thought I should come here when I wouldn't have to drag her along. You know she usually complains about traveling." He looked anxious. "You said I could come. Is it not a good time for you?"

Jon felt bad. His father always worried about causing someone a problem. "I'm delighted, Dad. But I haven't bought another bed for the apartment. Don't worry. I'll get one before I go back to the clinic."

"Can you do that?" His father asked.

"Sure," Jon responded. "Rawhide has most everything a person could need."

Raising one eyebrow, Tori said, "Sounds like you've changed your opinion about Rawhide since you first arrived, Doctor."

"It does, doesn't it," Mr. Wilson said.

"I guess he shared his attitude toward small towns before he left Chicago," Tori said with a smile.

"Call me Bill. I was hoping he'd change his mind after he got here. This town looks like a nice place to live, especially with pretty girls like you two."

"Thanks, Bill. Call me Tori, and this is my sister Jessica."

"I can't believe it, Dad. Aunt Tabitha never does anything without you. What happened?"

"She goes to lunch a few blocks away once a week with an old friend. Of course, I have to get the car out and drive her, but I don't mind. Only this time, her friend offered to pay for Tabitha to go with her as a companion on a cruise to Alaska. To my surprise, Tabitha agreed and packed overnight. I figured it was my opportunity to see the mountains."

"I'm glad you came, Dad." Jon smiled at his father.

"And you're right. The mountains are beautiful,"

Tori assured him. "We'll have you out to the ranch to get a closer look at them."

"A real ranch?"

"Yes, a real ranch," Tori assured him.

Tori enjoyed their lunch and the give and take between Jon and his father. They were obviously close. She was sure Jon missed his father. But, like him, she would miss her family, too, if she moved away. It didn't change her mind about anything, but Chicago really wasn't the problem. Whether Jon loved her was the problem.

Tori and Jessica had finished their meals. Nodding at her sister, Tori asked Jon to let her out at the same time Jessica made her way past Bill. "We enjoyed sharing lunch with you, Bill, but we've got to get back to work. I'm sure we'll see you soon."

Bill stood, then leaned toward Tori. "You're not going to help us shop?"

Tori smiled. "We really should get back to the office."

"But we'll see you when you come out on the Fourth," Jessica said. "We're having a big party on the Fourth. You'll meet a lot of people. And most of them will be kin to us."

"That sounds mighty fine," Bill accepted after a quick look at his son. "Are you sure you don't need to go back to work, Jon?"

"I'm sure, Dad. Tori, couldn't you and Jess accompany us? We'll go to Megan's store and shop."

"Who's Megan?" Bill asked.

Tori chuckled. "Another of those Randalls, Bill. You'll run into us everywhere."

"Well, if they're as nice as you two, I'll be happy," he said gently, smiling.

Tori decided he was a sweetheart.

Jon grabbed the check and went to the cash register to pay. Tori followed him. "I'll pay for mine and Jess's lunch, Jon."

"Nope. You rescued Dad. I should have checked my messages last night, but I wasn't expecting any calls. I have a beeper for medical emergencies."

"Your father is very nice."

"He worries too much."

"We're delighted to welcome him."

"Yeah. I'm glad."

"Yes, but I wanted to talk to you about putting your arm around me in public."

"I don't think it hurt anything. And it felt good."

She couldn't deny his statement, because it had felt good. Too good.

When they stepped out of the café, they discovered Jessica and Bill walking down the street toward Megan's store.

"Where's Jessica going?" Tori asked, distracted from their conversation.

"Looks like she's escorting Dad to Megan's. Do you think she'll have anything to sell me?"

"Maybe. Sometimes she takes regular furniture in, like your table and chairs. When you get there, tell Jess to come back to work, okay?"

"Why don't you come with us? I bet you worked all morning without a break."

"Of course I did. After yesterday, I had plenty of work stacked up."

"You can at least take an entire hour for lunch. Come with me, please?"

She was clearly wavering and he pressed her. "Please? And I'll need to buy sheets and stuff. Where will I get them in town?"

"Jennifer can help you with that. They carry bedding."

"I'm not going in there without you!" Jon exclaimed, showing a ridiculous fear that made Tori laugh.

"You're being silly."

"Yeah, but I still want you to come with me."

She sighed. "Okay, for a few minutes. Then I have to get to work."

He agreed, feeling lucky to get her to spend any time with him at all. They started down the street, hand in hand, until she realized he was holding her hand. She yanked hers away and put some distance between them.

Chapter Thirteen

Tori saw Bill Wilson the next day. She liked Bill and wasn't upset about his appearance. Especially since Jon wasn't with him.

Tori was afraid she was letting down her guard with Jon too much. But he was hard to resist. So it was better if she didn't spend any time with him.

Since July Fourth was on Monday, the weekend before that day was to be spent preparing. The office would be closed for three days. Tori explained to Bill that she spent Friday putting in long hours at the office.

Both she and Jessica had greeted him with a smile when he'd wandered down around noon, but they both continued working. Tori was concerned about getting more work done so Russ wouldn't feel overwhelmed by what needed to be accomplished when he returned to work. Jon had warned her that Russ wouldn't be able to put in a full day.

The problem for Tori was struggling to keep up with her own work, with all the interruptions and changes in her life.

"I know I'm in the way," he said softly, "but I don't know what to do with myself. Can I help you in any way?" he asked.

Jessica told him he could file for her, but Tori stopped her. "Jess, that's your job. What else would you do?"

Jessica shrugged. "I know, but I hate filing."

"I'll do it for you, Jessica. You and your sister have been so nice to me."

"Don't be silly, Bill. We're nice because you're nice," Jessica told him. "I'll be ready for lunch in a few minutes. Why don't you sit down and wait?"

Bill agreed and settled in a chair by Jessica's desk. Tori returned to her office and the work that awaited her. Half an hour later, Bill knocked on the wall, standing in the doorway. "Are you ready for lunch, Tori?"

She didn't even turn around. "Give me five minutes, Bill, and I'll have this account finished." She didn't even hear him answer or realize he'd moved closer to her, her concentration was so deep.

"I've never seen that software before. What's the name of it?"

Tori, surprised, turned to look at Bill. "What? You haven't seen—what do you do for a living, Bill?"

"I'm a bookkeeper," he said. "I shouldn't have disturbed you. I know how it is when you're concentrating."

"That's all right. You haven't seen this before because I developed it by taking the software my father developed for ranch accounts and applying it to retail.''

''Your father developed software for accounting? I look forward to meeting him.''

Tori jumped up, catching Bill's hand and tugging him after her. ''Come see.'' She led him into Russ's office. She turned on his computer and pulled up the software Russ used. ''See how this works?'' she asked, going over different aspects with Bill. He seemed fascinated.

''This is excellent, and very easy to use.''

''Do you think so? Too bad you're on vacation. We could use some help,'' she admitted with a chuckle.

''I'll be glad to help. I have nothing to do.''

''No, of course not,'' Tori said. ''It's your vacation.''

''But, Tori, I have nothing to do. I cleaned Jon's apartment, but when I finished, it was only ten o'clock. I sat there watching that little bitty television, but I couldn't stand it for long.''

''Would you really like to work? I can pay you an hourly wage.'' She mentioned an amount much more than he normally made, and his eyes widened.

''Money isn't necessary.''

''Yes, it is, Bill. If you could work this afternoon, and anytime next week, after Monday, of course, I'd love for you to help us out.''

''You've got a deal,'' Bill agreed with a big grin.

Tori hugged his neck to say thank you. Jessica had

reached the door and protested. "Hey! Tori, Bill is my beau, not yours. You've got Jon!"

"Don't be silly, Jess. Bill is our friend. Do you think Jon will mind?" she suddenly asked.

"Oh, I forgot." Bill frowned and Tori thought she'd lost his assistance.

"What is it, Bill?"

"We can't tell Jon."

Tori stared at him. "Why not?"

"Because he would think he needed to entertain me. And then I would feel I needed to go back to Chicago so I wouldn't be in his way." He paused, then added, "I like it here."

Tori was ready to argue with him, uncomfortable with lying to Jon, when they heard Jon's voice in the outer office.

"Hey? Where is everyone?"

Jessica turned around and greeted him.

Tori leaned close to Bill and said, "We'll talk after lunch."

Bill nodded. Then he went into the outer office to greet his son.

"How are you, Dad? I thought you'd sleep late today, but the apartment is spotless."

"I slept a little late, then cleaned. I just came down a few minutes ago. Tori's been showing me their software. It's amazing."

"Good, I'm glad they were entertaining." He leaned over and brushed his lips on Tori's cheek. "The Randalls are wonderful people."

Tori was fighting the shivers that ran through her,

and the urge to throw her arms around Jon as she had earlier hugged Bill. She drew a deep breath and stepped toward the door, hoping to find a safe distance from Jon.

"Ready for lunch?" Jon said, and Tori assumed he was talking to Bill.

When no one else responded, she looked up to find Jon watching her. "Oh! You mean us, too?"

"Of course. I owe you lunch just for entertaining Dad. I know you have a lot of work to do."

"Uh, yes, but he didn't—we enjoyed his visit." Mercy, she wasn't used to keeping secrets. She was afraid to say anything in case she slipped up. It would be so perfect if Bill could do a lot of work for Russ.

"I'm glad. He's a pretty good guy," Jon said with a big grin on his face. He seemed to be in a happy mood. "Let's go eat. I was trying to figure out what to do to entertain Dad. Can we discuss some things over lunch?"

Tori carefully looked away from Bill. "Of—of course, Jessica will have a lot of ideas, but I'm going to stay here and work. She'll bring me something back."

"As your doctor, I don't recommend that. You need to take a break." He took both her hands in his.

"I'll take a break after we catch up," she promised him. "Russ will be getting out of the hospital on Tuesday. I don't want him overwhelmed."

Jon looked over his shoulder at their audience. "You two go ahead and order me the special, whatever it is. I'll be there in a minute."

Jessica urged Bill to walk with her.

Jon smiled at Tori. "Everything all right? You seem tense this morning."

"Tense?" Tori jumped. "No! Not at all. I'm—I've been working hard all morning."

"Yeah, too hard," he said. "Are you sure you won't join us?"

"No, thank you, I can't. Just remind Jessica to bring me my salad when she leaves to come back."

He leaned over and brushed her lips with his. "I hope you're noticing how agreeable I'm being. But be sure to eat your lunch."

"I will."

"I don't want to leave you here."

"You're being ridiculous, Jon. No doctor should monitor his patients as much as you. I'll be fine." At least she would be when she got some distance from him. If she let him know how she felt about him, he would insist they marry if she was pregnant. But she wouldn't submit her child to a marriage of convenience that would be very inconvenient to her.

She wanted her husband's love, not his duty.

"If you want to eat alone with your father, you can tell Jessica I said for her to get both our lunches to go and come back to work." Maybe that was why he was lingering.

"Nope. I could bring *my* lunch back here and eat with you."

"No! No, then I wouldn't get any work done."

"You're right, and too beautiful to be an accountant.'' He tugged on her hands, trying to pull her closer.

''Jon, go have lunch with your father.'' This time, she tugged on his hands, moving him toward the door. As she pushed it open for him, Jennifer Waggoner came to the door.

''Tori? Hi. Are you going to lunch?'' Jennifer called out, smiling at Jon even though she spoke to Tori.

''No, but Jon is. Would you like to join him? You met Jon's father yesterday, didn't you?'' Tori asked, feeling she was babbling. But she was glad to have Jennifer take her place. She needed something to stop the growing hunger she felt for Jon Wilson. Had that been why the minutes in his arms had felt so right, so perfect, when they'd scarcely spent time together?

''Why, thank you. I'd love to.'' Jennifer slipped her hand through Jon's arm as if he were escorting her, which made Tori happy, she promised herself. She tried to ignore the protest that rose in her, *No, he's mine!* But she'd told everyone he wasn't.

WHEN THEY REACHED the café, Jon discovered Jessica and Bill already in a four-person booth. As if she were shocked, Jennifer said, ''Oh, I didn't realize—Jon, why don't you and I take one of those two-people booths over there, so they won't have to move. You don't mind, do you?''

Jon had no intention of having a private lunch with Jennifer. He said, ''I'd like to have lunch with my dad. He'll have to go back soon.'' He knew Jennifer had been trying to cut him out of the herd as neatly as the most talented cowboy. It wasn't the first time. When she pouted at his refusal, he shrugged his shoulders.

After they sat down, Jessica asked, "Bill, you met Jennifer last night, didn't you?"

Bill greeted her politely, but he sent a questioning look at Jon that Jon tried to ignore. He'd have to explain later.

Jessica then asked, "Where's Tori?"

"She decided to stay and work. She wants you to bring her a salad."

"Sure, in fact, I think I'll order my food to go, too. We've got a lot of work to do," Jessica said, smiling at Bill. "You don't mind, do you, Bill?"

"No, of course not, but—I guess I'll see you later."

Even as Jessica slid out of the booth, Jon stared at his father. "Uh, Dad, we'll go explore this afternoon, if you want. Tori and Jessica really do have a lot of work to do."

"Oh, I'll go with you!" Jennifer suggested.

"You don't have to work?" Jon asked, frowning. He didn't want to deal with Jennifer all afternoon.

"Sarah won't mind. She likes to work," Jennifer assured him with a smile.

"Well, you two go exploring if you want. I was thinking about taking a nap this afternoon. I don't usually have the chance to do that."

Jon stared at his father again. He'd never heard his father talk about taking naps. Was he aging more than

Jon had thought? "Are you feeling all right, Dad? I can give you a checkup if you want."

"An afternoon of looking around might be too much for him, Jon. I can show you everything and you can take him another day." Jennifer looked at him in anticipation.

She sounded more insistent than Jon liked. "No, Jennifer, we'd better not go today. Thanks for the offer, but—"

"I know. You're too busy. I'm beginning to get the message. In fact, I think I'll go without lunch, if you don't mind. Please let me out."

Jon stood. After Jennifer had huffed her way from the restaurant, Jon sat down again. "Looks like it's just you and me, Dad."

Bill nodded. "Jennifer's a pretty woman."

"Yeah, but Tori's prettier."

Bill sighed. "I'm glad to hear it. Jennifer is flashier, but Tori has a bigger heart."

"You were fast to pick up on that. I didn't see her heart at first. I saw the blond hair, her petite build, and thought she was like Mom."

"Your mom wasn't all bad, but I'll admit she got rather difficult toward the end."

With a sigh, Jon said, "That's an understatement."

"So, do you and Tori have an agreement?"

Jon shrugged his shoulders. "I wish."

"Don't worry son. I'm sure it will work out."

WHEN JON LEFT the clinic that afternoon, he felt guilty about working a full day while his father sat at home.

Tomorrow was Saturday. He'd take his father and drive toward the mountains.

He got to his apartment only to find it empty. He assumed his father was walking around town. He walked a lot in Chicago. Instead of going to look for him, he changed into jeans and a shirt, fixed himself a cup of caffeine-free coffee and sat down at the table, thinking about Tori. It had been a week since the trip up into the mountains. He had another week to wait until he'd have to insist Tori take a pregnancy test.

After a week of trying to grow closer to her, he knew he'd made a little progress. But that only created a problem. The closer he got, the closer he wanted to get. The woman was incredible in looks, in intelligence, in sweetness, in sexiness—whoa! There was his problem. He wanted her. He was beginning to think he wanted her for all time.

He was shocked at that thought. He felt a second shock when he realized he didn't want to leave Rawhide. The fresh air, the friendliness of the people, the sense of space, all impressed him, without even counting in Tori's presence. And he'd admit that being the only doctor for the town, even with Doc Jacoby still around, was flattering.

He felt as if he was already a part of the fabric of life in Rawhide. He was looking forward to the party at the Randalls. They had done a lot for him.

Thinking back to his arrival, determined to keep a distance from everyone, expecting his belongings to be stolen, he'd been a real pain. Yet everyone had been so good to him. And continued to be.

His dad should get to know everyone. He'd really love it here. If he had something to do. He was too young to retire. Maybe he'd like to work at the feed and general store. Would he like that? Today, when he'd offered to take off work early, his father had said he was looking forward to a nap.

Maybe his father was more tired than he realized.

Maybe a grandchild would make him younger

A smile played around Jon's mouth as he thought of petite Tori big with his child. He realized how much he wanted her to be pregnant. But he didn't want her to marry him for the sake of the child. He wanted Tori's love.

But he'd also committed himself to his father.

Rawhide, Wyoming, was a great place to live…if he could talk his father into moving Aunt Tabitha here. He'd have to talk to him about that possibility.

The apartment door opened and his father came in, freezing when he saw his son. "Oh! You're home."

Jon frowned. "Yeah. Where have you been?"

"Oh. Around. This is a nice town."

"I was just thinking that. I thought I'd hate it, but—you're right. It's a nice town."

"It's even better with Tori here," Bill added, beaming at him.

Jon couldn't hold back a grin. "Yeah."

"So when are you going to marry?"

"Uh, I told you, Dad. We haven't discussed it yet. You wouldn't object to my marrying her?"

"Hell, no. She's a sweetheart. And sharp! She

showed me the software, you know. It's great. They could sell that program and make a fortune.''

"I understand she does all right in the stock market, too. She's got an uncle who's a stock whiz and he's been teaching her."

"You'd better catch her before someone else does.'' Bill fixed himself a cup of coffee, too, and sat at the table. "Which reminds me, what do you have planned for tonight?"

"Uh, nothing, Dad. There isn't a movie house or anything here."

"No, not for me. I'm happy to just sit and talk, but it's Friday night. Doesn't Tori expect you to spend time with her?"

Jon thought about Tori's possible reaction to that question. "Uh, no, I hadn't made any plans for tonight."

"Well, you should. You *will* lose her if you don't."

"We watched a movie on television the other night. Why don't we do that?"

"On that little bitty television?"

"No. Tori has a nice-size television. We could ask her to let us join her. I could go buy some steaks and cook them over there. What about that?"

"That's a good idea, but don't count me in. That wouldn't be romantic!"

"Dad, we want you to share the evening with us. In fact, I'll run to the grocery store before it closes. You go arrange everything with Tori while I buy some groceries." He wanted to kiss his dad. He hadn't figured out a way to see Tori this evening.

Now his father would ask, and he knew Tori wouldn't refuse.

"Well, okay, but I don't want to be in the way."

"You won't be, Dad."

"BUT MOM," Tori began to protest.

"Where are your manners, young lady? Jon's father has come to visit and you don't want to invite them to dinner?"

"Mother, if you want to call Jon and ask him and Bill to dinner, that's fine. There's no reason for me to be involved."

She held her breath, hoping her mother would buy that argument.

Her mother calmly said, "I'll expect the three of you to be here at seven. I think Rich and Samantha and Lavinia will be here, also."

Before Tori could protest, her mother said goodbye and hung up the phone.

"Oh, great. This is all Jon's fault!"

She gave in, as she'd known she would, and lifted the phone again, calling Jon next door. It would be easier to extend the invitation on the phone. She might even get to talk to Bill instead of Jon. Bill, who didn't embarrass her, tempt her or touch her.

Bill answered the phone.

"Hello?" His voice was very hesitant.

"Bill, it's Tori."

"Tori! I was just coming to see you," he said, sounding more confident. "Jon has gone to the grocery store to get steaks. We'll cook dinner if we can watch television at your place. You know, Jon's television is terrible.''

"I know." She cleared her throat. "But those plans won't work."

Before she could explain, he asked, "You've got a date with someone else?"

"No, Bill, not at all. But my mother called and invited the three of us to come for dinner at the ranch. Would you like that?"

"At a real ranch?"

"Yes, Bill, at a real ranch."

"You know, I think I'm really going to like it here in Rawhide."

Chapter Fourteen

After dinner that night, Tori began clearing the table, following the rule that the children cleaned the kitchen, when she noticed that her father and Bill had their heads together. Brett loved numbers and accounting, and his brothers looked upon it as a necessary evil. Now he had Tori to talk to, and Russ, but no one his own age.

"Hey, Jon, looks like your dad and Uncle Brett are hitting it off," Casey pointed out.

"Yeah. It's real friendly of Brett."

Tori hadn't realized Jon was staying in the kitchen. She whirled around. "Why don't you join them, Jon? After all, you're a guest." She'd be able to breathe much better with him out of the kitchen.

He stepped to Tori's side. "You telling me I'm too old to help out?"

Desperately afraid he'd kiss her again in front of all her cousins, she ducked away from him and headed to the sink with her stack of dishes. "No, of course not."

"Not too old, but you're a doctor," Jessica pointed

out. "So you don't get to wash. We don't want your talented hands to shrivel up," she added with a grin. "What do you choose, loading the dishwasher or wielding a mop?"

"You organizing us, Jess?" Elizabeth asked in surprise.

"The sooner we get finished, the sooner we can go into town," Jessica pointed out. "I've got a new outfit I intend to show off. Hopefully, it will impress a certain man I've got my eye on."

Everyone laughed, with a shout or two of "Go for it, Jess!"

Elizabeth smiled at her with a touch of pity. "That's just a meat market, Jess. You can do better than that."

"I don't know," Jessica teased. "I think Toby showed his face at the 'meat market' a few times."

"So did Elizabeth, I do believe," Toby pointed out. "She almost drove me crazy."

Though her cheeks were red, Elizabeth moved into her husband's arms and said, "Good."

Jim, Elizabeth's brother, one of Chad and Megan's two sons, protested. "Don't get mushy in here, you two. Go talk with the others. We'll finish the cleanup."

Toby cocked an eyebrow. "You're heading into town, too, I suppose."

"Yeah," Jim admitted with a grin.

Elizabeth said, "I've got a better idea. As soon as the kitchen is mopped and the food put away, why don't you all go ahead? Toby and I will finish here."

Several people cheered and worked faster.

Toby protested, but everyone knew he was teasing. "Where are Rich and Russ when I need them? They already have—" He stopped abruptly and the kitchen grew deadly silent. "Sorry," Toby mumbled. "I forgot."

In an attempt to divert everyone's attention, Tori said, "I'll be glad to help, Elizabeth."

"Thanks," Elizabeth said, "but you should go kick up your heels, Tori. You've had a rough time lately."

"They have dancing?" Jon asked. "I didn't realize—"

"You like dancing, Doc?" Jim asked, relief on his face as the awkward moment passed.

"I've been known to dance a little. Of course, I don't know how to line dance. Is that what you do here?"

"Sometimes," Jim agreed, "but it's easy."

"Yeah, maybe I can get Tori to teach me."

Tori discovered everyone in the room staring at her.

"You'll find lots of ladies willing to teach you," she assured Jon stiffly. "I'm going to stay here."

JON IMMEDIATELY GOT CLOSE to Jim and quietly suggested that he convince Tori to join the group going to town, adding that she needed to have fun for a change.

He was relieved when Jim accommodated him. Because the thought of dancing with Tori almost had Jon tongue-tied. The idea of holding her close, putting his arms around her, feeling her body touching his, brought a hunger so intense he was afraid his body might betray him in front of everyone.

And he knew Tori would refuse to go if he was the one pressing her.

Fifteen minutes later, it was settled. Tori had agreed to go. Jon had been careful to keep a low profile. But he slipped into the living room to tell his father he was going to town with the other young people and would be back in a couple of hours. If he didn't want to wait that long, Bill could go with Jon.

Brett looked at him. "Jon, if you're going with our kids, I wouldn't count on being back in a couple of hours."

"Nope," Jake added. "Our kids party hard, just like they do everything else. Why not let Bill spend the night here? You can bring him some fresh clothes early in the morning. In fact, you should both stay the weekend. We're going to give Bill some riding lessons."

Jon stared at his father. "Dad? What do you want to do?"

His father was embarrassed by his question. "I don't want to cause any trouble. I can go back now and have you drop me off at the apartment."

Jon studied his father. When he'd come in, he'd noted how comfortable his father was with these men. Contrasting that to the picture of his father sitting in the apartment alone made Jon decide what to do. "I'll be out early with some clean clothes, Dad. Don't get on a horse until I get here. I need a few pointers, too."

The light returned to his father's eyes. "You're sure it's not too much of an imposition?" he asked Brett.

After being reassured, Bill told Jon he'd see him in the morning and showed no anxiety at being abandoned. Jon almost chuckled aloud at that thought. As if his father were a child.

He returned to the kitchen.

"They're waiting for you outside," Elizabeth told him. Toby grinned in encouragement and waved him through the kitchen to the outside. He hurried. He wasn't going to miss his opportunity to dance with Tori.

When he got outside, he thought the others had left without him. He stood there, trying to think what to do, when Casey, the twins' younger brother, called to him. "Come on, Doc. I'm your guide."

He hadn't seen the boy in the shadows, but Casey was waiting by Jon's SUV. With a grin, he ran for the driver's seat and they were on their way.

"Not that you really need a guide, 'cause there's only one place to go. Nothing else is open, except for the café until nine. Then it's closed, too."

"Did Tori go with the others?" Jon asked, wanting to be sure she'd be there.

"Yeah. But I told her I'd wait for you."

Jon didn't tell Casey he'd have preferred Tori's company. But it was best that she went with someone else. It gave him time to get his body under control.

The bar and restaurant, a steak house, wasn't too far from his apartment. "Are the steaks good here?"

he asked Casey, thinking he needed to bring his dad
here for dinner one night.

"Yeah, but that's not what we came for," Casey
reminded him, waggling his eyebrows.

"You've got a special lady?" Jon asked.

Casey's grin widened. "Several."

Jon couldn't help himself. "You are responsible,
aren't you?"

"Yeah, *Dad*, I'm responsible."

"Sorry, I know it's none of my business." Not
only was it none of his business, but he hadn't taken
his own advice, which made him ashamed.

"It probably is, since the consequences might in-
volve you, but our parents have drilled that into our
heads. But I'm not—I mean, I haven't—I like dancing
with girls."

Jon grinned. "Good. So do I."

"You'll get your chance tonight."

TORI HAD JUST FINISHED assuring a handsome cowboy
that there was nothing between her and the new doctor, when Jon walked in. She knew at once he was
there.

She quickly looked away and asked the cowboy
about a local rodeo coming up soon.

He expounded on his entries and his chances for
several minutes, but Tori didn't hear much. Fortunately, an occasional word kept him going for a
while, until the music ended.

They turned to leave the dance floor and she came

face-to-face with Jon. "Oh, hi, Jon. Have you met Yancy Brown?"

Jon extended his hand and nodded to the cowboy.

"Good to meet you, Doc. Might come in handy since I'm going to bull-ride in the Buffalo Wild West Rodeo next week."

"Ah, sounds exciting."

"It can be," the cowboy said with a grin.

Jon decided he liked the man in spite of the fact that his arm was still around Tori's small waist. When the music started again, he quickly said, "Hope you don't mind if I borrow your partner." He didn't wait for the man's agreement as he pulled Tori into his arms.

"As long as you bring her back," Yancy called after him.

Tori had said nothing, because she hadn't realized Jon's intention. Now she protested, "I don't believe you asked me."

"Madam Honey, will you dance with me?"

"Gee, a girl loves to dance with someone who doesn't know her name," Tori teased, smiling at his ridiculous form of address.

"Oops. I made a mistake. It must be Madam Sweetheart. Or sugar-pie. I heard your mother call you that tonight. I like that name."

"Only mothers get to use those absurd words."

"When you're a mother, will you use it?"

Those words reminded her again of their past. She immediately tried to put some distance between them.

Distance she could admit to herself she didn't want. But she couldn't tell Jon that.

"Whoa! Where are you going?"

"I—I didn't want to crowd you," she mumbled.

"Crowd away, sweetheart. You can't get too close for me."

"Jon—"

"I'll behave, Tori, I promise," he quickly said as she started to leave him. "You were dancing closer with that cowboy than you are with me."

"He's an old friend."

"I thought maybe we'd become friends this week. I've tried to get closer to you. That's what your cousins reminded me of. That we put the cart before the horse," he said, suddenly serious.

So that had been what her cousins said. She'd wondered. Her respect for them grew, because they were right. There had been so little between Jon and her— no memories, nothing in common. Well, a little, but not enough to bring them to such intimacy.

So why did she long for him to make love to her again? A few lunches, watching a movie with a chaperon, meeting his father. Even now, they were only at the beginning of a friendship, much less—

"Yes, we're friends, but not lovers," she said firmly, trying to belie the feelings she could admit only to herself.

"Good. That means we can dance a little closer." He pulled her against him and she gave up protesting. She was enjoying being close to him too much.

JON WASN'T SURPRISED when Tori refused the next dance with him. She wanted to keep people from talking. He knew he'd have to pace himself with her, but he didn't want to. He didn't want her in another man's arms. She was his!

He sighed. Damn weird time to realize that. But he knew the feeling had been growing in him all week. If he hadn't made love to her in the cabin, he'd be hot on her trail now, hoping to. But he figured it would be a long time before she'd trust him that much. Maybe not until their wedding night.

He returned to the big table the Randalls were occupying. Casey and Josh, Jake and B.J.'s youngest, though he was older than Casey, were sitting there along with a lady. Jon recognized Sarah, Jennifer's sister, and greeted her.

She responded, but with a lot of reserve.

"How about a dance, Sarah? I don't know many people here, especially pretty ladies," Jon said with a smile.

There was a silence that told him she wasn't anxious to accommodate him, but she finally agreed.

Once they started dancing, he said, "Unhappy with me?"

Her head jerked up and she stared at him. "I don't appreciate your hurting Jennifer."

He frowned. "I had no intention of hurting her. How did I do that?"

"She made it obvious she was interested in dating you and you rejected her."

Jon figured that was Jennifer's interpretation. "I'm

sorry, but I had already—I'm interested in someone else. Jennifer is a beautiful young lady, as you are, but when you fall for someone else, what can you do?''

"Tori?''

Jon nodded. He knew Tori would be upset if she heard him, but he didn't care. He wanted everyone to know he wanted her. Particularly every cowboy in the state.

"Oh.''

They danced in silence. Then Sarah said, "Tori is a good friend. I'll tell Jennifer. She'll forgive you then.''

Jon said, "I don't believe I need to have forgiveness for following my heart.''

"You don't understand. Tori was matchmaking when she brought us into the picture. Jen thought she was doing Tori a favor.''

"I understand that, but I think your sister got her nose out of joint because I didn't fall at her feet.''

"Of course she did. Men do that all the time.'' Sarah paused, then added, "I know she's a little spoiled, but she's very beautiful.''

"Doesn't it happen to you, too?''

"No, of course not,'' Sarah said, dismissing such an idea.

"Sarah, I think you sadly underestimate yourself.''

She smiled. "No, Jon, I learned to face facts a long time ago. Jen has always been the pretty one. I've been her protector, like her mother, since our mom died when I was eight. Dad's gone now, too, so I'm the only one left to take care of her.''

Jon was astounded. Sarah talked as if she were a parent. "How much older are you than Jennifer?"

"Three years. I'm twenty-eight."

"And who takes care of you?"

She appeared startled. "Why, me, of course. I'm fortunate that I have a good head for business."

The music ended, and Jon asked, "Friends?"

"Friends," she agreed, a charming smile on her face. Jon decided she was worth a lot more than her sister. He admitted Jennifer wasn't a bad sort, but, as he'd suspected earlier, she was spoiled. When push came to shove, maybe she'd be as worthy as Sarah.

But he wanted Tori. He took Sarah back to the table, where Jennifer, surrounded by several cowboys, was standing. She gave him a cool nod and then smiled at one of her companions. Jon smiled at Sarah. "I'm glad we got to visit."

Tori approached the table with her partner. She wanted to talk to Sarah, but Jon didn't think that was a good idea. Besides, he wanted her back in his arms.

"I think this is a line dance, Tori. You said you'd teach me," he reminded her.

"I don't think—" she began, but he pulled her after him, not having really seen denial in her eyes.

"Jon, we can't dance every dance together," she whispered.

"I know. Just every other one."

She choked, but he loved the sparkle in her blue

eyes. Then he wrapped his arms around her, drawing her close.

"I thought it was a line dance, not a two-step. We're supposed to dance apart."

"I was wrong."

She didn't say anything, but she also didn't protest anymore, and her body was touching his.

"Did you enjoy your dance with Sarah?" she finally whispered.

That remark told him she'd kept her eye on him. He kissed her neck in reward. "Very much so, after we cleared up a little problem."

"What problem?" She eased back a bit to stare up at him.

But he wasn't telling now. He had to keep her intrigued with something so he could take her home, without anyone chaperoning them.

"We'll talk later. I think it's important and I can't concentrate with you in my arms."

She stared intently at him, then, in answer to his prayers, laid her head on his chest and danced.

He did a good job keeping her away from Sarah the rest of the evening, helped by willing cowboys. After their third dance together, interspersed by several cowboys, she confessed she was too tired to dance anymore.

"Ready to go home?" he asked, enjoying the sound of those words.

"Yes, but I can walk. There's no need for you to leave. I'm sure there are lots more women anxious to dance with you."

"You know better," he said, chastising her gently.

"Truly, Jon, I'm sure—"

"You know better than to think I'd stay here when you're leaving." He continued to dance close to her until the end of the song. He wasn't going to give up time with her in his arms. But as soon as it ended, he took her hand. "Come on, let's go tell the others we're leaving."

Jennifer was again at the table, still standing, and stared at their linked hands.

"Jon," she acknowledged, as if he meant nothing to her. Which suited Jon just fine.

"Want me to find you a partner?" she asked, as if only her help could save him from being a wallflower.

"I appreciate that, Jennifer, but I'll have to take a rain check. We're wiped out from our busy day and are calling it an evening."

"We?" she questioned frostily.

"Tori and I. Or is it me?" he asked the others with a grin. Before Jennifer could say anything else, Jon told the others they were leaving and he'd see them tomorrow.

Jim looked at Tori. "You okay? Are you coming out tomorrow?"

"Yes, of course. Mildred wants me to help with the cookies, so I'll be slaving in the kitchen all day."

He grinned. "That's probably more fun than rounding up some of Uncle Pete's bulls for our mini-rodeo."

Tori smiled. "I know the cookies smell better!"

"Yeah," he agreed. "Save me a few." Then he

looked at Jon. "You getting her home safely?" he asked, as if he was responsible for Tori.

"Yeah. I'll take care of her." Jon stared at Jim and the man nodded back.

"I'll count on it."

Outside, Jon decided to walk the two blocks to their apartments, holding Tori's hand. It would lengthen their time alone together before he had to say goodnight. She made no objection when he suggested it. It seemed her mind was on other things.

"What was that exchange you had with Jim?"

"In my estimation," he said with a grin, "he was questioning my intentions. And my integrity. And sending a little warning."

She protested, "That's not necessary."

"Yes, it is. It's man talk. You don't understand."

"Man talk?" she said with disdain. "I don't think so!"

Jon lightly squeezed her hand.

They walked along in silence, drawing farther away from the bar's music and the crowd. The moon was rising in the east, and Jon thought again that Rawhide was a nice place.

"What did you mean about the dance with Sarah?"

"Hmm, it seems she's very protective of Jennifer."

Tori sighed. "I know she is."

"Well, she didn't think I was a nice man because I hadn't fallen at Jennifer's feet." He grinned at Tori.

"What did you tell her?"

He didn't hesitate. "I told her I was too distracted by you. It was all your fault."

"Jon Wilson! How dare you blame me! I haven't—"

He pulled her against him and covered her protest with his lips. The need to kiss her deeply, to become one with her, to never let her go, overpowered his good sense.

He didn't think she was ready yet to hear what he wanted to say. She was still fighting him on the possible pregnancy. He thought he should wait until that question was answered before he expressed his feelings. But his body wasn't interested in waiting.

She pushed away from him, out of breath. Instead of protesting, as he expected her to do, she whirled around and hurried toward her apartment.

He followed, easily keeping up with her but not touching her. He'd pressed her too hard, too fast. But damn, it had felt good.

Neither spoke until she got to her door.

"We need to talk," he protested, not letting her close the door behind her.

"About what?" she demanded as she spun around to glare at him.

"About Jennifer…and about tomorrow."

"Jennifer thought she was doing me a favor. She's unused to having her advances rejected, but she's good at heart. And there's nothing to talk about tomorrow. I'm going to the ranch to work. I don't care what you do."

"Are you driving or am I?" he asked, as if everything was settled to his satisfaction.

"*I* am driving *myself*," she said, leaving no room for discussion.

"Okay, I'll ride with you."

"No, Jon, we are not a couple. Drive yourself." Then she started to close the door.

Just as his beeper went off.

She opened her door again. "What was that?"

"My beeper. May I use your phone?" He could have as easily unlocked his door and used his phone, but he didn't want to.

She stepped back and waved him past her.

He dialed the clinic number. "This is Dr. Wilson." He listened intently, then said, "I'll be right there."

"What is it?" Tori asked as soon as he hung up.

"A little boy with a possible appendicitis. I've got to go."

He bent down and briefly kissed her, like a husband off to work. She didn't even protest.

"Your car! It's at the bar and the clinic is two blocks in the other direction." She grabbed her keys and added, "Come on, I'll drive you."

He didn't argue, following her down the stairs. After all, driving would have him there faster.

"You can call me when you're ready to come home and I'll pick you up," she added.

"No, that won't be necessary. It could be a while and you're already tired."

"That doesn't matter. Do you get a lot of calls at night?"

"All the time in Chicago, but I was working ER.

Not as often out here, but it seems to be a rule of thumb that children only get sick in the dark.''

She pulled up in front of the clinic. "Do you need any help?"

"No, I want you to go to bed and get some rest. You try to do too much." She started to protest, but he leaned over and kissed her again.

"Thanks. I'll see you in the morning."

This time she didn't protest.

Chapter Fifteen

Jon rolled out of bed the next morning at seven-thirty. He'd gotten home from the clinic about two, so he hadn't gotten a lot of sleep. First he called to check on his little patient, but the nurses reported the boy was awake and happy.

"I'm going to be out at the Randall ranch. Just beep me if you need me."

"Of course, Doctor."

After hanging up, Jon hurried to the window to look out at the parking lot. He could see Tori's compact sedan in its usual spot. She hadn't left without him. He needed to shave and shower, but he'd check with Tori first.

Pulling on a pair of jeans and a T-shirt, he hurried next door and rapped softly. No answer. He knocked louder. Her car was there. She must be, too.

Finally he made a fist and pounded on the door.

"I'm coming!" a sleepy voice called out.

She'd still been asleep? He'd gotten her home last night before eleven. She must have really been tired.

Like a pregnant woman.

His breath caught in his throat. As he was warning himself not to make a big deal out of her oversleeping, she opened the door just enough to see who was there.

"What is it?" she demanded in a grumpy voice.

"I thought I was late and wanted to tell you I'd be ready to go as soon as I grab a shower."

"Ready to go?" She stared at him.

"You're not awake yet, are you?" he asked, smiling. He leaned forward and kissed her lips. He didn't know about her, but that action certainly woke him up…all over.

When he finally lifted his lips, Tori was in his embrace, her arms around his neck.

She stared up at him, her breathing rapid. "You— shouldn't do that." Something caught her eye over his shoulder. Suddenly she leaned to one side to see behind him and gasped. "Jon Wilson, I cannot believe you pulled me out onto the balcony in front of the entire city in my nightclothes."

Heck, he hadn't realized he'd done it, either. "I thought you were dressed," he protested as his gaze roamed her body. A soft T-shirt seemed to be her only piece of clothing. For a petite lady, her body was perfectly proportioned with comparatively long legs. A tempting sight.

She shoved at him. "Stop looking!" Then she spun around and ran for her bedroom. She entered the bedroom and slammed the door behind her.

He followed her in. "When will you be ready to go?"

"I've got to shower and dress!" she replied through the door.

"I don't suppose you'd consider conserving water by sharing your shower?"

The bedroom door opened, like the front door, only a few inches. She remained behind the door. "Jon Wilson, get in your own shower. You have fifteen— no, make it twenty—minutes if we're going to ride together to the ranch." Then she slammed the door again.

With a grin on his face, he jogged back to his own apartment.

He was even faster than she'd ordered. Dressed in clean jeans and a plaid shirt, tennis shoes on his feet, he hurried across to the café and ordered two cinnamon buns to go and two cups of hot coffee. He'd picked up his car last night, so he unlocked it this morning and put the food inside. Then he locked it again.

When he got back upstairs, Tori was knocking on his door.

"Ready?" he called.

"Where have you been?"

"To get a surprise for you. Come on." He took her hand, which was becoming a habit, one he enjoyed. He escorted her to the front passenger seat of his SUV. He was tempted to pick her up. She smelled so sweet, so fresh, so…delicious. But she jumped in before he could do so.

When he got in, she was beaming at him. "Coffee and cinnamon buns! I could kiss you, Jon!"

"I sure won't stop you," he promised, and leaned forward.

She dropped a light kiss on his cheek and sat back.

He cleared his throat and forced himself not to grab her. "I would have thought you could do better than that for a hot cup of coffee."

She grinned. "I'm not at my best in the morning."

"I think I know how to change that," he said.

"Hmm?"

"Aren't you going to ask me how?"

"No, I'm not, and I don't want you to tell me, either. We're almost to the ranch and I haven't even had a chance to eat my cinnamon bun. I've learned the hard way that you don't bring other people's food and eat it in front of Red and Mildred."

"Good point. Pass me my cinnamon bun."

BY MONDAY, July Fourth, everything was ready. Even the animals had been rounded up for the rodeo, which would take place that afternoon. Jon had gone home each night during the preparation, but, to his surprise, his father did not.

Bill seemed very comfortable with the Randalls.

Jon now knew he'd probably stay in Rawhide, an unbelievable realization when he'd first arrived. But he hadn't known he would fall in love, something he readily admitted now. He believed the quality of life in Rawhide was better than in Chicago. He wanted his family to stay.

But a happy vacation didn't mean they would be happy there forever. He would wait until the end of his father's vacation and ask him how he felt about Rawhide.

Most important, however, was Tori and how she felt about him. He'd been encouraged by her acceptance of his touch. She smiled, laughed and watched him. The weekend had been delightful because they'd spent time together. Saturday they'd gone their separate ways, him to the corral where his dad was riding a horse for the first time. She'd headed for the kitchen to make a million cookies with Mildred.

At least she'd said it seemed like a million cookies. He'd tasted a few on the way home and told her she'd done a great job. On Sunday, he'd helped the men set up tables and benches in the grassy area by the barn with the arena, where the rodeo would be held in the afternoon, followed by a barbecue buffet, fireworks and square dancing.

He dressed and called Tori. "Are you awake?"

It sounded as if she was stretching as she answered him, and his mouth watered with hunger to hold her. "What time is it?"

She was definitely in her bed. He pictured her in that soft T-shirt, her legs bare. He shook his head, hoping to dispel that picture. "It's eight-thirty."

"Oh, I can sleep a little longer."

"Okay. I'm going to the clinic to check on a couple of patients, but I'll be back about nine-thirty. How about breakfast at the café when I get back? Then we can go to the ranch. Deal?"

"Mmm-hmm," she agreed, and hung up the phone.

Jon sat there with a smile on his face. Someday

he'd be able to awaken her with a kiss, not a telephone call. Maybe, for the rest of his life.

He forced himself to head for the clinic. When he took care of his business there, he'd be able to return to Tori.

TORI SNUGGLED back down under her blanket, a smile on her face. Jon was going to take her to breakfast. She was beginning to get used to starting her day with Jon. She liked it too much.

If, as she'd maintained all along, she wasn't pregnant, she wouldn't receive the attention she was getting now. Jon appeared to be one of those honorable men who took responsibility for his actions.

As long as he thought she was pregnant, he would court her. And he was very good at it. If she didn't know better, she would believe he loved her…as she loved him. But she hadn't forgotten his reaction when he realized they hadn't used protection.

The harshness of his voice, his abrupt response, told her what he felt. She had to keep remembering those moments. But it was getting more and more difficult. Because she wanted to believe he loved her—wanted to but couldn't. Not until she knew if there was a baby. She couldn't risk her heart. She believed if he knew there was no baby, he would walk away, free to return to Chicago.

"Well," she muttered, "I've managed to ruin my day with those depressing thoughts." She shoved back the blanket and headed for the shower. She might *be* depressed, but she wasn't going to look depressed today at the big party…or at breakfast with Jon.

When she'd styled her clean hair, dressed in new jeans that fit her snugly and added a red, white and blue T-shirt, she turned to her makeup. Then she put on gold hoop earrings.

It was nine-fifteen, a quarter hour before Jon would show up. She wrote a brief note, "Meet you there," and taped it to his door. Then she strolled across the street to the café.

She was really going to have to get herself under control. When she proved she wasn't pregnant, she wanted to be strong. To show Jon that she didn't blame him for his pursuit of her.

What she wanted to do was fall into his arms and beg him not to leave her. But that wasn't going to happen.

Maybe he'd make up with Jennifer. She was probably the prettiest woman in Rawhide. Men always noticed that. And Jon was definitely all man.

"Morning, Tori. You alone this morning?" Mona asked. "I've gotten used to seeing you with that good-looking doctor, you lucky lady."

"He's coming, but that will change soon, I'm sure. He's going to meet a lot more people at the party today. He's been busy and hasn't met too many people, you know."

"I can believe every single woman around will be after him. Aren't you worried?"

"No, of course not. We're just friends, Mona. And

I imagine we'll be friends for four years. That's when he's leaving.''

''I've heard, but I've also heard Doc's planning on marrying him off to a local so he'll stay.''

''Or take her with him to Chicago,'' Tori pointed out. ''I can't imagine it, but there might be some ladies willing to move on. But not me.''

''Oh, I see,'' Mona said, a sad look on her face. ''Too bad.''

Tori hoped Mona believed her. But she admitted to herself, if Jon loved her, she would go wherever he went. Something she'd never believed she'd do.

''Um, is this booth all right?'' she asked, changing the subject.

''Sure, hon. Wherever you want. We're not very busy this morning.''

Tori slid into the booth, facing the door.

Almost as soon as she sat down, the door opened and Jon came in. He walked immediately to her side of the booth and bent over to kiss her.

When he stood up again and slid in the other side, Tori found Mona grinning at her, as if to say, *Yeah, sure, just friends.*

''Were you starving, sweetheart? Sorry if I took too long.''

''Did you have a problem?''

''Not really. Just a couple of patients wanting emergency care.''

''Your life is never your own, is it?'' she asked with a frown.

"That happens when you're the only practicing doctor in town. Does it bother you?"

She snapped her head up. "Not me! It has nothing to do with me." She had to make that clear.

Jon raised one eyebrow, which only increased his sexiness. "I see. Well, I guess it's true, but I took the Hippocratic oath to help others. And fortunately, I get paid for doing my duty. A little inconvenience isn't so bad."

"Okay, you two, what'll you have?" Mona asked.

He waited for Tori to order, but she'd lost her appetite. "I guess I'll have coffee and a cinnamon bun."

"You're going to make me feel bad. I'm starving. I'll have the all-American breakfast, Mona. I need lots of energy for the party. Are you coming?"

"You bet. The boss shuts down during the Randalls' party 'cause everyone else is there. Are you riding?"

Jon stared at her, his mouth open. Then he looked at Tori. "Is she serious?"

"I think so," Tori said, laughter in her voice.

"Don't you ride?" Mona asked, her voice rising in surprise.

"I'm from Chicago, Mona. Sure I've ridden a horse, a couple of times for an hour each. Ask Tori. When I went up the mountain with her, I couldn't walk when I got back."

"So I guess you'll watch."

"Yeah, and help repair any damage those guys cause."

"Oh, I hadn't thought of that."

Jon handed her his menu. "I'm starving."

Mona apologized and grabbed the menus, hurrying to the kitchen.

"Is everyone supposed to ride in a rodeo? I heard someone say Pete and Toby both did that, but—"

"And Rich, though he didn't last long. He broke his ankle, and then he got smart and came home with Samantha."

"Samantha isn't from around here?"

"No. But it seems like it now. It's like she's always been a Randall." She paused, then added softly, "Like Abby."

"Yeah." He reached across the table to take her hand in his. "Samantha's doing well, sweetheart. What happened to Abby is rare."

She didn't say anything.

"Our baby will be born safely. Don't worry."

She couldn't stop herself. "There is no baby!"

"You've been sleeping a lot lately. And you threw up the other day. You've been a little cranky, too. Especially early in the morning." He grinned at her. "If you're not pregnant, take a pregnancy test next Monday."

She looked away. So much for being cheerful.

Mona delivered their choices with a smile.

Tori began to pick at her cinnamon bun and drink her coffee, knowing Jon was watching her. "Fine, I'll take the test next Monday." And then her contact with Jon would be over. She started sliding out of the booth.

"Where are you going?" Jon demanded, alarm on his face.

"I'm going to visit the ladies' room, if you don't mind."

"Nope, I don't. Frequent urination. Ask any pregnant woman."

So HE'D CONVINCED HER to take the pregnancy test.

At the price of her disappearance. Oh, she hadn't really disappeared. But now she was distant, silent, frowning. And as soon as they'd gotten to the ranch, she'd suddenly become busy.

He'd joined the men, helping with a few things. But now, the people were beginning to arrive. Hordes of people. "I didn't know this many people live in Rawhide," he muttered to Toby.

"They don't. A lot of them live on ranches. Not only the owners, but also the cowboys. And a lot of them will be riding in the rodeo. You might get to meet them up close and personal," Toby assured him.

"Were you ever injured when you were on the rodeo circuit?"

"Nothing serious." He turned and then grinned. "Here come the ladies. I'd better grab Elizabeth. She draws men—like honey draws bees. In fact, all our ladies do, except maybe Sam. Six months pregnant kind of scares some guys. Or maybe it's Rich's obvious annoyance that scares them." He chuckled.

Jon had been scanning the ladies who were carrying food to the picnic area. Finally he found Tori's pale blond hair. It was because she was shorter that he hadn't seen her at first. "I'll go with you," he told Toby.

When he reached Tori, however, she wanted nothing to do with him. He couldn't figure it out. Was it because she thought he didn't trust her? That was silly. *She* didn't know if she was pregnant. It wasn't a matter of trust.

He followed her anyway.

After she'd put a dish of food on one of the serving tables, she turned around and headed for the house.

"Wait, Tori. Tell me what's wrong."

She stared at him, her gaze cool and bare of emotion. "Nothing's wrong." She started to walk again, but suddenly someone grabbed her waist and swung her around. Fierce anger was on her face until she realized who had her in his grasp. Then she threw her arms around the man's neck.

And Jon wanted to punch him out.

"Gabe! I didn't know you were going to make it!" Her smile was glorious. Jon was sure he was a brilliant chartreuse with envy, hating this Gabe's gut.

"Come with me. I have to make another trip. You can help." She grabbed the man by his hand and hurried toward the house.

Jon wanted to protest that he'd offered to help first. Why hadn't she greeted him like that? He was the father of her baby, after all.

He grabbed Brett, who was standing nearby. "Brett, did you see the man who went to the house with Tori?"

"No, I didn't. Is something wrong?"

"She greeted him like she—she loved him."

"And how's that?"

"He picked her up and she threw her arms around his neck and invited him to go to the house with her."

Tori came out of the house at that moment with the handsome stranger beside her, each of them carrying a dish.

"There! There he is."

"Hey, it's Gabe!" Brett shouted, and hurried over to welcome the man, followed by the other brothers and some of the cousins, too.

"Damn it, what's going on?" Jon mumbled to himself.

"What is it, son?" his father asked. "Something wrong?"

"Yeah, something's wrong. Tori welcomed that stranger as if he were her lover!"

"I'm sure you're wrong. Tori seems like an angel, an honest angel."

"WHO'S THE GUY who keeps glowering at me?" Gabe asked Tori.

She didn't bother to look up. "I don't know what you mean." She studied the bowls on the table and decided to rearrange them.

"I don't mind fighting for your reputation, you know, but I'd like to be prepared. Seems to me he's in love with you."

"No, he's not."

"So, who is he?"

"The new doctor."

"Really? He might come in handy if I get hurt today. Maybe I should meet him," Gabe suggested, watching Tori closely.

"Suit yourself," she said, shrugging her shoulders.

Gabe wrapped his arm around Tori and began walking toward the doctor.

"Turn me loose, Gabe. *I* don't want to talk to him."

"But I need you to introduce me. Or I could ask someone else in the family to make the introduction…and ask them why he's upset with me."

"No! I mean, fine. I'll introduce you."

They'd reached Jon, and he was still glaring at Gabe.

"Jon," she acknowledged tersely. "This is Gabe. He wanted to meet you."

She tried to run away, but Gabe kept hold of her. He stuck out his right hand to Jon. "Gabe Randall. Glad to meet you."

Jon didn't move, but the glare turned into a frown. "You're a Randall?"

Gabe lowered his arm. "Yeah. You got something against the Randalls?"

"No. Are you her brother?"

"Nope. A cousin, sort of."

"Sort of?"

"What's wrong with you, man?" Gabe finally asked.

"I don't like to see my woman hugging another man."

Gabe stared at him, then Tori, and back again. "You mean Tori?"

"I think she's the only lady you've got your hands on," Jon pointed out.

Gabe roared with laughter. "Tori, what have you been up to?"

"Nothing!" she snapped.

"You have nothing to worry about from me, Doc. I treat Tori like my little sister. But for a lady you're claiming, she seems a mite unhappy to see you."

"I know, and she won't tell me why." With his eyes, Jon pleaded for an explanation, but Tori wouldn't even glance at him.

Then someone called Tori's name. All three of them looked toward the area where the cars were being parked. Two ladies, one brunette and the other a beautiful blonde, were hurrying in their direction.

Gabe stiffened. "Who's the blond goddess?" he asked intensely.

"That's Jennifer, isn't it, Tori?" Jon answered, pleased to see the interest in the other man's gaze.

"You know her, Tori?" Gabe asked.

"Yes."

"Good. Introduce me."

Jon stuck out his hand. "Glad to meet you, Gabe Randall. He smiled for the first time. "Welcome to Rawhide."

Chapter Sixteen

The party was over.

And a grand party it had been. Other than scrapes and bruises, Jon had had only one real patient. A young man had broken an arm when he was tossed from the back of a nasty bull.

But Jon had hoped for so much more.

True, he'd met a lot of people. Nice people. And the Randalls had almost treated him like family. His father had had a grand time, helping release the bull and rider from the chutes.

Tori still wouldn't talk to him.

Talk? Heck, she wouldn't come within a hundred yards of him. And she'd disappeared about an hour ago and hadn't been seen since. He caught a glimpse of Anna. "Anna? Have you seen Tori?"

She stopped and turned around to gaze at him, a sad expression on her face. "She's inside. I sent her to bed a little while ago."

"But I thought she was going back to town with me."

"She decided to stay here tonight. Sorry if she forgot to let you know."

Instead of thanking her and walking away, Jon said, "You know why she's upset, don't you?"

Anna nodded.

"Aren't you going to tell me? How can I fix it if I don't know what's wrong? Anna, this is important. Tell me!"

"I can't do that, Jon. You're on your own." Then she went into the house.

He followed her in, not because he thought she'd change her mind, but because his father had gone into the house earlier. "Dad?" he called, when he caught sight of Bill. "You ready to go?"

"Sure, son."

"Aren't you going to stay, Bill?" Brett asked.

"No, thanks. I've made plans in town tomorrow." He grinned. "But hopefully I'll be back out before I have to leave."

"We think you should move out here," Chad said. "We'd love to have you as a neighbor."

"I can't retire just yet, Chad, but thanks for the kind words."

Jon scarcely noticed his father's conversation. His mind was on Tori and the need to touch her again, to be sure she was all right, to make her happy.

The drive home was silent. Jon didn't notice. He kept thinking about what had gone wrong. When they got to the apartment, he went to bed because he couldn't think anymore. It was too depressing.

TORI HAD TOLD HER MOTHER the truth. How she'd come to love Jon, but she knew he wouldn't be interested in her once he discovered she wasn't pregnant. And she'd promised to take a pregnancy test next Monday.

She got up and dressed in the clothes she'd worn yesterday and had breakfast. Her mother was going to drive her into town.

"Mom, let's stop at the drugstore. I'm going to buy a pregnancy test today."

"Won't it be too early?"

"No, I don't think so. And I can't live an entire week waiting for the ax to fall. I want to get this misery over with."

"Have you considered the fact that you might be pregnant?"

Tori sent her mother a sad look. "No, because I'm not. And even if I am, I can't marry Jon. It would be like trapping a wild animal and trying to make it a pet. He would never be happy. And neither would I."

"I'll go in and buy it."

Tori didn't argue.

Her mother came up to her apartment when they got there. She waited with Tori when she took the test. Then she held her in her arms as Tori sobbed when the test showed negative.

Finally, when Tori seemed under control, Anna got up to leave.

"Mom, are you going to the clinic?"

Anna nodded.

"Will you take a note to Jon?"

"Of course, dear."

Tori wrote a brief note to Jon and included the test results in an envelope. After sealing it, she handed it to her mother. "Just give him this."

Her mother gave her a hug and, taking the envelope, she hurried to her car.

It took Tori a little while to repair the damage to her face. She thought Bill would be downstairs with Jessica, and she didn't want him to know anything was wrong. When she got there, Bill and Jessica looked up and greeted her.

"Sorry I'm late," she said briefly, and headed for her office.

"Tori?" Jessica called. "What's wrong? It's not Russ, is it? Isn't he getting out of the hospital today?"

So much for fixing her face.

"Nothing's wrong. I'm sure Russ will go straight to the ranch today, Jess. He'll be there when you get home. Or if you're anxious to see him, you can go home at lunch."

Jess continued to stare at her and Tori bit her bottom lip, hoping to hold back the tears.

Bill came closer. "Is there anything I can do, Tori? I've made some progress today. I hope that helps."

She patted him on the arm. "Of course it helps, Bill. I know Russ will appreciate all your hard work."

Inside, she was screaming, *Leave me alone!*

Then Bill, who was facing the front door, said, "Look, there's Jon with Russ now. He's here, Jessica!"

Tori slipped into her office and closed the door.

JON WAS GLAD Russ was showing an interest in his business. It was a sign of good mental health. And it also gave him a chance to see Tori this morning.

He'd wanted to call her, but she wasn't at home.

Jessica and his father met them at the door. His father? Jon looked at his watch. It wasn't even ten o'clock yet. He was going to have to speak to his father about not spending so much of his time in Tori's office.

"Who is that with Jessica?" Russ asked.

"My father."

Russ gave him a strange look but only said, "Oh."

Jessica hugged Russ when they got to the door. Then his father introduced himself, shaking Russ's hand.

"Where's Tori?" Russ asked, looking over their shoulders.

Jon wanted the answer to that question, too. "Maybe she's not back from the ranch?"

Jessica turned around, then faced Russ and Jon again. "Um, she's back. I think she had something really important to work on, um, didn't she, Bill?"

All three men saw the plea in Jessica's gaze.

Bill immediately rushed to support her. "That's right. I think she had to, er, check some figures for me," he said, a triumphant smile on his face at having come up with an excuse.

Jon's gaze narrowed. "Why would her work have anything to do with you, Dad?"

"Because I'm doing—" He stopped abruptly, his gaze widening in guilt. "Er, I asked her a question."

"A question more important than my arrival?" Russ asked indignantly. "Something strange is going on." He started toward Tori's office.

Jon followed until Jessica grabbed his arm. "Don't, please, Jon. Something *is* wrong, but we don't know what and she'll be embarrassed if you see her cry. Tori almost never cries."

"She's been crying this morning?" Jon asked rapidly.

"We—we think so," Jessica said. "She didn't admit it, but she looked terrible, didn't she, Bill?"

He nodded his head.

Jon switched to another topic while he waited for Russ to reappear.

"Dad, I know you like Jessica and Tori, but you're going to have to stop interfering with their work. I'll find you something to do, somewhere to visit, or I'll take a couple of days off. Doc will fill in for me."

"No, he can't do that!" Jessica exclaimed.

"Why not?"

Tori's door opened, which distracted Jon at once from his father's activities. "Where's Tori?"

"She's working. She's gotten behind and has to get something out right away. Let's go to the café and have a cup of coffee," Russ suggested.

"But Tori should—"

"Jon, she'll feel much better when she gets this job done. Maybe she'll even join us. Come on, I need to sit down."

"I'd better stay here," Jessica said with a grimace.

"No, honey," Russ said gently. "Tori insists you go, too."

"But she might need me."

"I think she needs to be alone." Russ took Jessica's arm, and added, "You can help a cripple across the street." As soon as he'd convinced Jessica, he gestured to Jon to precede him. "And you too, Bill. We've got some talking to do."

Bill's face took on an anxious expression as he walked out the door. Jon followed, since Russ had given him no choice. But he wanted to stay behind and confront Tori—right now, however, he guessed he'd have to apologize for his father's behavior. And figure out what to do with him.

As soon as everyone left the office, Tori grabbed her purse and pulled out her car keys. Then she picked up the phone and called the clinic. "Mom, did you give the note to Jon?"

"Yes, honey, but I didn't tell him it was from you. He was going to take Russ to the ranch, and he said he'd read it when he got back."

Tori drew a deep breath, a shaky deep breath. "Okay. I'm going to drive into Casper and do some shopping."

"Casper? What are you shopping for?" Casper was a two-hour drive away. Usually they only went to Casper for something terribly important.

"My peace of mind," Tori whispered. "I'll be back this evening."

"Want to stay at the ranch?"

"No. This is my home now, and I won't be driven out of it. But I need some space before I'm strong enough to stand firm."

"All right. If we can do anything, let me know."

"I will. Thanks, Mom." She'd always been grateful that her parents let her fight her own battles, but they always let her know they were there if she needed them.

She slipped out of the office and hurried to her car. Once inside, she locked her doors and drove away.

JESSICA AND RUSS WERE sitting in the booth facing the street and both saw Tori drive away. Jess looked at him, but Russ shook his head. Tori had given him a thumbnail sketch of the difficulty.

He liked Jon. Not only was he a skilled doctor, but he was also a man who cared about his patients, just the kind of doctor they wanted. But if it was a choice between Jon and Tori, he'd come down on Tori's side. She was family.

"I want to apologize for my father constantly interrupting your work, Jessica. I'm going to take a few days off to entertain him, so—"

"No, Jon, you can't," Russ said calmly.

Jon stared at his friend. "What are you talking about?"

"I need Bill. He promised to help get me caught up until he leaves. I think he's happy with that arrangement, aren't you, Bill?"

Bill looked absolutely hangdog, but he nodded.

"But, Bill, if you want to do things with Jon instead of work, it's okay, you know,'' Russ added, not sure now that the older man liked the arrangement.

''Wait a minute!'' Jon barked. ''Are you telling me my father is working during his vacation? He's supposed to be relaxing.''

Bill said nothing.

Mona, who'd taken their orders and brought cups and saucers and a pot of coffee, came back to the table. They all sat silently while she filled the cups. Then she delivered their cinnamon buns.

It had given Jon time to think. ''Are you liking the work, Dad?'' He tried to keep any judgment from his voice.

Bill perked up and said, ''It's great! Tori and Jessica are fun to work with, and I love the software Russ uses. I feel like I'm doing real work. I really—'' He stopped, his face stricken. Then he began again in a sedate manner. ''It gives me something to do while you're at work, son.''

Jon ran his hand over his face and condemned himself. ''I see. I should've done a better job of paying attention.''

''No, no, you're fine, Jon. You're the best son there is!''

''Thanks, Dad, but you're blind to my faults, and I have a lot of them.''

Bill began to protest, but Jon shushed him. ''Russ, how much longer will you be able to use Dad's help?''

''We can use him as long as he's willing to work,''

he said. "I know he's supposed to go home on Sunday, so—"

Jon grinned. "No, you don't understand the question. Is there a chance for permanent employment with you?"

"Heck, yeah! Tori says he's great. We've been thinking about taking on some help, but the job pool in Rawhide is kind of small. Especially for people with his skills," Russ explained.

Bill's expression was anxious and eager at the same time.

"You mean, Bill might stay?" Jessica asked excitedly.

"If he wants to," Jon agreed.

"Well, of course he wants to!" Jessica exclaimed. "Rawhide is much better than Chicago. Right, Bill?"

"Right!" Bill agreed, beaming. "Do you think I can move here, Jon? It won't upset you? And what about Aunt Tabitha?"

"Dad, the only reason I was coming back to Chicago is because of you and Aunt Tabitha. I wanted to make sure you were happy. We'll tell Aunt Tabitha she can move in with her friend, or come here. We'll find her a place to live."

"Tabitha seems to like being with her friend."

"Well, we'll give her a choice, Dad. I'd be delighted if you moved here."

"I can't believe this is happening," Bill exclaimed.

"Will Tori object?" Jon abruptly asked.

It was Jessica again who answered. "Of course not. She loves Bill!"

Russ shrugged.

Jon slid out of the booth.

"Where are you going, Jon?" Russ asked.

"To talk to Tori."

"She's not there. She left a few minutes ago."

"Where'd she go?"

"I don't know. She told me she needed to be alone."

"Well, damn it, that's not what I need!"

"Did you get her note?" Russ asked.

Jon froze, staring intently at Russ. "What note?"

"She said she sent you a note with Anna."

Without a word, Jon raced out of the café.

IT WAS AFTER EIGHT when Tori parked in the back of her apartment. She didn't get out of the car until she'd checked to be sure Jon wasn't around. Then she scurried up the stairs to her apartment, quietly slipping in. Not exactly the brave front she'd promised herself.

She made a quick call to her mother to let her know she was home, but she didn't have a conversation, really. Then she undressed and grabbed a quick shower. She was exhausted. And looked it, she decided, staring into the mirror in the bathroom.

She had circles under her eyes and she was too pale. Maybe the fact that she hadn't stopped for dinner had something to do with it. Or maybe it was lunch. The day had slipped away. She hadn't done any shopping. She hadn't had the heart for it.

She'd asked herself the question, "What am I going to do for four years?" over and over again. Maybe she'd take a boat to Australia, and tour that country for six months. She had enough money.

But why spend it when Australia wouldn't look any different from Wyoming? Not because it really was like Wyoming, but because she wouldn't be looking. Or she could open a branch office in Buffalo. Far enough away not to see or hear about Jon, but close enough to see her family occasionally. Yes, that would be a better choice. She couldn't give up her family.

She'd have to wait a week or two to talk to Russ about it. It would help if Bill could remain working for them. Then it wouldn't be so hard on Russ.

She was too tired to think anymore tonight. She was going straight to bed. As Scarlett said, "Tomorrow is another day."

And she was right. But there was no guarantee it would be a *better* day.

Dressed in one of her long T-shirts and panties, she pulled back the cover on her bed, just as the pounding started on her door.

She knew who was there. Jon would want to properly express his sentiments. She'd like to ignore him, but better to let him get the words out tonight, than to fear facing them tomorrow.

She slipped on a robe and went to the door. "Who is it?"

"You know who it is," he said calmly. "Open up, Tori."

After a moment, she did so.

Without words, he pushed past her and pulled out a chair at her table.

She remained by the door. "Come right in, Jon. It doesn't matter that I'm ready for bed. Of course I want to talk to you."

"Good."

With a sigh, she closed the door and came to the table, noticing for the first time that he carried a grocery sack. "It's not necessary to bring food every time you— Of course, I don't need to tell you that, because you won't be coming over anymore."

"Why not?"

She was trying to be strong, but he wasn't cooperating. "Didn't you get my note?"

"Yeah. Wasn't it a little early for the test?"

"I'm not pregnant! You're free to go on with your life! Got that, Jon?"

He looked at her solemnly, and she couldn't stand it. She turned away, crossing her arms over her chest. If she didn't, he would see her trembling hands. "You need to leave, Jon. Our conversation is over."

"What conversation? Sit down, Tori. I brought a snack."

He opened his sack and reached in.

"I don't care what you brought, Jon. I want you to leave. I can't—"

She stopped, because she saw what he put on the table. Ice cream and pickles. Typical pregnancy food.

"Damn it, get out! Stop tormenting me! Just go—" She couldn't believe she had any more tears to shed, but there they were again, streaming down her cheeks. "I'm—not—pregnant!"

He stood up and took her into his arms. She was too weak, too distraught, too everything to protest.

"I know you're not, sweetheart. I thought we'd get a head start on next time." He squeezed her closer to him. "Only this time, we'll get married first."

Standing in his arms, hiding her face in his shirt, it took several minutes for his words to penetrate her grief. Finally she raised her tear-streaked face and stared at him. "What did you say?" she asked, hiccuping.

"I said what I've been trying to say for a long time. I love you. I think I've been in love with you since I first saw you, but then I made love to you too soon, and it messed everything up."

"That's not true! When you realized—at the cabin, you were—you don't, either!"

"I made a mistake. I was stunned by our lovemaking, sweetheart. It was so incredibly powerful. Then I realized what I'd done. I'm a doctor! I preach about unprotected sex! I even said something to Casey the other night. But *I* didn't practice it? With you? I risked hurting you? I was furious with myself, not you. When we made love, I didn't want to let you go. And I've been trying to find a way to get close to you again ever since."

"You could've told me!" she protested, still frowning but no longer crying.

"You've got to be kidding. You wouldn't talk to me. You hardly even looked at me. So I tried to find out about the baby. That made you furious. I didn't know what to do.''

She buried her head in his shirtfront. ''I—I wanted the baby. I was so sad when I took the test.''

''I should have been here with you, sweetheart, but you shut me out.''

She backed out of his arms, her hands on her hips. ''How was I supposed to know it mattered to you?''

''I don't know, since you wouldn't share your feelings with me.''

''Oh, so I'm supposed to share while you hide your feelings? I don't think so.''

He grinned. ''Couldn't you tell I love you? That Gabe Randall made me sick to my stomach, until Jennifer came into the picture? I'm grateful to her, now.''

She gave a watery chuckle. ''He was smitten, wasn't he? I hope Jennifer is sweet to him. Gabe hasn't had a happy life. I want someone to love him.''

''Do you think Jennifer is the kind to be there for someone else?''

''I think she can be. Anyway, Gabe will be around a lot to see Jennifer, he said, so I'm glad you don't hate him.''

''As long as it's Jennifer he wants to see, he's welcome anytime. What's one more Randall?''

''Jon,'' she said then, her voice wobbling. ''Are you sure?''

''Yeah, I'm happy about Gabe and Jennifer.''

''No! I mean about—about loving me?''

He pulled her back into his arms. ''As sure as I am

about staying in Rawhide, with you, for the rest of my life."

"But—but you said you were leaving in four years."

"If I did, would you go with me?"

She didn't hesitate. "Yes. I'd rather stay here, but, yes, I'd go with you."

Now there were tears in his eyes. "I love you so much. But I won't ask that of you, sweetheart. I was going back to Chicago for Dad and Aunt Tabitha. But Dad has been caught up in the magic of Rawhide and he wants to stay as much as I do. We're going to make arrangements with Aunt Tabitha."

He kissed her once, and then continued reslanting his mouth over hers to get closer, covering her soft skin with his hands, sliding them under her T-shirt, finally exploring the secrets it hid.

Until something plopped on his shoe.

"Oh, dear," Tori exclaimed, breathing shallowly, "the ice cream's melting!"

Jon picked up the carton and put it in the sink. Grabbing a paper towel, he wiped up the soggy mess left on the table. Then he swept Tori up into his arms and headed for the bedroom.

"Maybe if we put it in the freezer, it will keep," she said, looking over his shoulder.

"Don't worry about the ice cream, sweetheart. I'll buy more, along with the pickles, whenever you need them. And hopefully, it will be real soon."

Epilogue

"Anything else?" Jon called as he came in the front door.

"No, that's everything. I'm coming back tomorrow to make sure it's sparkling clean for Bill."

"Dad's real excited about having his own apartment," Jon said with a grin. His father might be excited, but not as much as Jon. He'd bought Russ's home from him. He and Tori, Mrs. Tori Wilson, were moving in today. They'd taken out the furniture Russ had left in the house and changed the decor. They didn't want Russ to avoid them because he couldn't bear the memories, but he'd helped them move some things in already.

He would never forget Abby, and Tori didn't want him to. But one day perhaps he could heal.

"Then let's go home, sweetheart," Jon suggested. "I want to continue our work on the need for ice cream and pickles."

Jon had moved into her apartment right away and they'd had a small wedding, as small a wedding as a Randall family wedding could be.

"We'd better. I want you to be able to carry me

over the threshold before I get so big you can't lift me,'' she said.

"Oh, we've got plenty of time," he said with a laugh.

"And you call yourself a doctor!" she teased.

Jon scooped her into his arms and started for the door but suddenly stopped, staring at Tori's smile.

"You're not!"

With big innocent blue eyes, she said, "Not what, dear?"

"You're not pregnant! Are you?"

"I haven't taken a test yet."

"Damn the tests! Are you?"

"I think so, but then I'm not a doctor!"

He kissed her with all his heart. He couldn't ask for any more happiness. His family around him—a much-expanded family—Tori in his arms and a child on the way.

When he'd borrowed the money for his loan, he'd never guessed he would get such happiness in return.

It was the best bargain he'd ever made.

* * * * *

The Randall family will be back
next month in Judy Christenberry's
original Harlequin single title,

UNBREAKABLE BONDS,

available in August, wherever
Harlequin Books are sold.
You won't want to miss the excitement
when Judy tells all about what
happened between Gabe and Jennifer—and
introduces a secret Randall twin!

HARLEQUIN®

AMERICAN *Romance*®

How do you marry a Hardison?

**First you tempt him. Then you tame him…
all the way to the altar.**

How to Marry A HARDISON

by
Kara Lennox

The handsome Hardison brothers are about to meet their
matches when three Texas ladies decide to stop at nothing
to lasso one of these most eligible bachelors.

Watch for:

VIXEN IN DISGUISE
August 2002

PLAIN JANE'S PLAN
October 2002

SASSY CINDERELLA
December 2002

Don't miss Kara Lennox's HOW TO MARRY A HARDISON
series, available wherever Harlequin books are sold.

HARLEQUIN®

Makes any time special®

HARHTMAH

Princes...Princesses...
London Castles...New York Mansions...
To live the life of a royal!

In 2002, Harlequin Books lets you escape to a world of royalty with these royally themed titles:

Temptation:
January 2002—*A Prince of a Guy* (#861)
February 2002—*A Noble Pursuit* (#865)

American Romance:
The Carradignes: American Royalty (Editorially linked series)
March 2002—*The Improperly Pregnant Princess* (#913)
April 2002—*The Unlawfully Wedded Princess* (#917)
May 2002—*The Simply Scandalous Princess* (#921)
November 2002—*The Inconveniently Engaged Prince* (#945)

Intrigue:
The Carradignes: A Royal Mystery (Editorially linked series)
June 2002—*The Duke's Covert Mission* (#666)

Chicago Confidential
September 2002—*Prince Under Cover* (#678)

The Crown Affair
October 2002—*Royal Target* (#682)
November 2002—*Royal Ransom* (#686)
December 2002—*Royal Pursuit* (#690)

Harlequin Romance:
June 2002—*His Majesty's Marriage* (#3703)
July 2002—*The Prince's Proposal* (#3709)

Harlequin Presents:
August 2002—*Society Weddings* (#2268)
September 2002—*The Prince's Pleasure* (#2274)

Duets:
September 2002—*Once Upon a Tiara/Henry Ever After* (#83)
October 2002—*Natalia's Story/Andrea's Story* (#85)

Celebrate a year of royalty with Harlequin Books!

Available at your favorite retail outlet.

Makes any time special ®

Visit us at www.eHarlequin.com

HSROY02

HARLEQUIN

AMERICAN *Romance*

and Debra Webb

invite you for a special consultation at the

COLBY AGENCY

THE MARRIAGE PRESCRIPTION
August 2002

Putting in too many long hours at the Colby Agency made firm counselor Zach Ashton…single! After his mother's recent heart attack, the workaholic bachelor felt compelled to return home for some R and R. But his plan didn't include acquiring a wife—until he reconnected with Dr. Beth McCormick, the girl next door. Trouble was, the good doctor was all woman now. Would Zach's remedy include .a marriage prescription?

HARLEQUIN
Makes any time special